ericka duffy • jane flett
nick holdstock • benjamin morris
jason morton • lauren schenkman
ryan van winkle
editors

stolen
stories

First published in Great Britain in 2008 by Forest Publications

First edition

10 9 8 7 6 5 4 3 2 1

ISBN-13: 978 0 9556456 1 7

Forest Publications
An Imprint of The Forest
Registered Office:
3 Bristo Place
Edinburgh
EH1 1EY
Registered at Companies House Edinburgh
Company Registration No. SC254177
Charity No. SC038234

Additional editorial support from Lyndsay Ann Bache
Ad [illegible] an
Co [illegible]
Art [illegible]
Ty [illegible]
Pri [illegible]

“N [illegible] t’s Tail
“Th [illegible]

stolen stories

stolenstories

Dedicated to the Forest volunteers.

stolenstories

introduction

Bad artists copy. Great artists steal.
Pablo Picasso

Fiction is, by definition, that which is 'made up'. Unlike biography, reportage, or booklets that purport to explain how to assemble your washing machine, fiction makes few claims to 'truth', not even the limited variety present in these genres. Which begs a couple of questions — how does a writer 'make up' something? — And what is the relationship between this construction and the truth? — the first of which we'll try to answer, the second of which we'll try to ignore.

When we, as writers, begin a story, most of us do so with an event, image, or psychological question we wish to explore. Sometimes there is only a title ('Richard and His Excellent Bears'), a first line ('Melanie refused to discuss her penchant for being inverted'), sometimes a last ('And with that the boy entered the deep, dark, dripping tunnel that led to the mine of adulthood'). All the above could be placed under the heading 'An Idea'. These are what people ask us about after we have given a reading. They march, totter, or are pushed to the mike, then after clearing their throats, croak, "Where do your ideas come from?" Usually we offer the same response given by Henry James in his 1908 preface to *The Portrait of a Lady*:

As for the origin of one's wind-blown germs... who shall say where they *come from. We have to go too far back, too far behind, to say. Isn't it all we can say that they come from every quarter of heaven, that they are* there *at almost any turn of the road? They accumulate, and we are always picking them over, selecting among them. They are the breath of life — by which I mean that life, in its own way, breathes them upon us. They are so, in a manner prescribed and imposed — floated into our minds by the current of life.*

Whilst this is enjoyably grand (not to say suitably mystifying), James' response, like our talk of first lines and images, is a form of evasion. To say that ideas come from 'every quarter of heaven' is little better than saying they come from the faeries, our 'collective unconscious', or a tiny green shoulder weasel that whispers ideas only we can hear.

The main items in 'the current of life' are people, who, as characters, are usually the main parts of a story. So a better question may be, 'Where do characters and their actions come from?' James suggests that 'life' gives them to us, but comes closer to the truth when he speaks of 'picking them over, selecting among them'. Our 'made up' characters and events are thus not so much given as *taken* from life. The writer's task is to select those parts of life he or she feels can be satisfactorily assembled into something as pleasing as a washing machine that not only makes one's clothes smell mother-laundered, but also never leaks in a manner that seems downright sorrowful. These range from the individual detail — a pencil-drawn eyebrow, the heft of a breast — to a particular face or way of speaking — pedantic, hectoring, a boiled sweet in the mouth — to a sketch of a person remarkable in its verisimilitude: one that captures the manner in which they laugh, dress, breathe, eat and fall down stairs[1].

None of this can be avoided. Writers are, after all, not God. We cannot create something from nothing. We are also not all-seeing: the majority of us are probably no more observant than average; certainly no more than policemen, pimps, or psychiatrists. When one considers the daily life of most writers — sitting in a room, perhaps the kitchen, often alone for most of the day — it becomes clear that the sphere from which most of us draw our 'wind-blown germs' is fairly limited. Those events and characters that interest us most are often drawn from family, friends, or colleagues[2], perhaps because we think we understand why ten-year-old Adam throws stones at dogs, why our friend Kirstey has yet to cheat on her husband, why Polly works so late, so

1 Booming; badly; from their diaphragm; messily; with grace.

2 Even Henry James, who had a remarkably wide circle of acquaintance — in London during the winter of 1878-9, he admitted to accepting 107 invitations — based many of his heroines on his cousin Minny Temple (e.g. Daisy Miller, Isabel Archer, and Milly Theale).

often, what she is avoiding at home. It may be that given our emotional connection to these people, their stories have a greater resonance for us, that they seem more deserving of being written, or at least included in our narratives. It is certainly easier than devising the inner lives of people who do not quite exist.

Which brings us to the nub of all this. For whilst there is nothing inherently problematic about placing one's girlfriend's nose in a story, fitting it, as it were, on another woman's face — not unless said nose is so malformed it resembles a whelk more than an organ of scent, such an inclusion calling further attention to an already sensitive matter — it is an altogether more fraught endeavour to place your actual girlfriend in a story, even under another name, with auburn hair rather than brown, but still with the same issues about your relationship, such as, for instance, her fear you'll leave for her for someone with a shapelier nose. Although it might be an excellent story, one of your best, it would cause her great suffering[3]. Amongst the many accusations she might later hurl as the two of you stand in the kitchen, you pressed against the washing machine, she leaning against the wall with the spice rack, the main point she might return to, as her hand sweeps the sage to the floor, would be that it was *her* nose and that you had no right to just *take* it and put it in a *story* for fucking strangers to *gawp* at. And though it was only a *nose*, for God's sake (and a horrible, mollusc-like one at that), by no means the most intimate detail you could

3 Whilst this is probably not among most writers' higher aspirations for their work, revenge as a guiding motive cannot be entirely discounted (cf. Philip Roth's *I Married a Communist*; Sylvia Plath's *The Bell Jar*).

have borrowed — not her baby-talk during sex; the way she snored like a vagrant; her habit of opening her mouth to show you the food she'd chewed — you would have to concede she had a point. You had taken, you had *stolen* something that did not belong to you.

Later, much later, after she had moved out, you might begin to question this notion. Although a person clearly 'owns' their own nose, can they be said to have the same rights of ownership when it comes to things they have said or done, especially if you were also present? What about *your* rights? After all, these were things *you* saw and heard. Surely that gives you the right to use them? But regardless of whether a person can truly 'own' their words, deeds and thoughts — in the way you still 'own' that Captain Beefheart record she took, even if you said it was a present — what is far more germane is that people *feel* they do. And it is they, rather than any abstract ethical or legal code, who matter. They are, after all — *pace* James — the proverbial hands that feed us.

The main issue is thus one of permission. This is the difference between borrowing and theft (at least when it comes to records). There is nothing to stop a writer from asking their partner, their colleague, or the girl on the no. 47 bus telling a long and impressively detailed account of what she did with a Cypriot waiter on Mykonos, if they mind themselves or their actions being included in a work of fiction. Nothing, I suspect, except the prospect of being told 'no' (and several other things besides[4]). Ideally, these people would instantly

4 Though let's face it, how many writers are going to take 'no' for an answer? It is as rhetorical a question as, "Do you mind if I have the last scone?" Or, "Do you mind if I take another breath of air?"

contract some baffling perceptual disorder unknown to clinical science, rendering them physically unable to read any story in which they or their actions appear. Given the likelihood of this scenario, most writers instead pile wigs and sweaters on the people in question, change their sex, nationality, and religion, or even split them into two or more characters, especially if they are writing something that shows the person (or their nose) in an unfavourable light. This, of course, does not always succeed. Some people are surprisingly acute at spotting themselves in fiction.

The other, somewhat safer option, is to portray the person in a manner unlikely to cause offense. Many of the stories in this anthology portray their subjects in a sympathetic manner, though this by no means guarantees a favourable reception, the most common accusation being 'that-isn't-how-it-was'. There are, however, several stories in the anthology ('Applesauce', for example) that gleefully announce their lack of shame at what amounts to a violation of trust, of telling a story those involved might prefer not to be shared.

We wish we'd been sent more stories like that.

Malice aside, perhaps what is most important is not a story's provenance, but how its author deals with the 'stolen' material. We were sent (and rejected) many stories that did little more than reproduce anecdotes. Some of which were so enjoyable — children whose glass eyes fall out, women who publicly insult each other's genitalia on a London bus, a man who claims to have 'built' the robot known (to the rest of us) as Naomi Campbell — we believe we could be forgiven for making a further volume of doubly stolen stories, if only because some of the 'wind-blown germs' we inhale seem to demand they be allowed to burgeon into a sickness (even when its prognosis is likely to be terminal[5]).

But however enjoyable or compelling the anecdote, what ultimately mattered to us during selection was how it had been transformed; how something overheard in a bar had been expanded into a structured narrative that did not merely tell you what happened, but gave you ways to think about it you did not expect, a piece of writing which, through its control of event and language, might affect you in some lasting manner — in short, how it had been made into a *story*[6].

Before we began putting this anthology together, few of us had doubted the ethics of appropriating from others' lives, probably because we never gave it much thought. A good story is all that matters, as journalists may still say. But in the end, if you write enough stories,

5 The question of why we are sometimes compelled to use a person, event, or nose is one that warrants further study. We would like to think that this urge, while not entirely philanthropic, is at least as public-spirited as the donation of one of those benches with a memorial nameplate. That we only use such material because we believe that its inclusion is fundamental to the world-improving quality of our work. We would *not* like to think of it as a piece of arch-selfishness, one wholly typical of us and our deceitful, treacherous, spiteful, self-centred, and thoroughly venal writerly ways.

6 The other main reason we rejected stories was that they took the 'sto len' theme as an excuse to make free with the writings of already-famous authors. Whilst there is nothing wrong with this — William Burroughs used to write 'GETS' in the margins of books, when he felt something was Good Enough To Steal — if you're going to tinker with the canon, it needs to be done not only outstandingly well (e.g. J.M. Coetzee's *Foe* or Jean Rhys's *Wide Sargasso Sea*) but also with a better legal defence than we would be able to muster.

someone will eventually say *J'accuse*. They will stand in your kitchen and ask by what right you took something *private*, something *shared*, and turned it into a *story*. They may be crying. So might you. But as you stare at their face, their unbelievable nose, you will realise that they will stand there as long as it takes. That they deserve — and you may need — some kind of answer to this.

Nick Holdstock
September 2008
Paris

introduction

applesauce

angus woodward

There are a lot of ways to not lie. It was not a lie when we said that we turned to Futons 'n' Things whenever we wanted sturdy, inexpensive furniture for cabins, dormitories, and starter homes, and that we had always known we could count on receiving only the best of customer service during our shopping experiences at Futons 'n' Things. We did not say that we had never owned a cabin, lived in dormitories, or purchased a starter home, or that we had never *consciously* associated great service with Futons 'n' Things.

I say "we" because I signed the letter that Phoebe typed on the laptop she had borrowed from her previous employer and never returned (not that they had asked her to return it).

The rest of the letter was just as truthful as that first paragraph. I don't remember the exact words we used, but the bulk of it described our visit to Futons 'n' Things that afternoon, described it in a certain light, that is — in the light one shines on such experiences in such letters, as in the letter that had gotten us a free night at Sunshine Inn after we found a caterpillar in our broccoli. The litter in the F 'n' T parking lot, the grubby glass of the front door, the long wait for Mr. Walker, the salesman, who did not even emerge from the back until we had been in the store for a full five minutes (not that we timed it, but in retrospect five minutes seemed a reasonable estimate). The fact that Mr. Walker (Tiger, as he introduced himself) wiped his hands on a dirty napkin as he emerged and failed to notice a falafel crumb suspended in his goatee the entire time we were there. His haughty correction of our pronunciation of futon, which we based upon our knowledge of Japanese (foo-TONE), not upon some crude Americanization. We liked the folding inner-spring double futon with the wicker frame and had even signaled to one another with our eyebrows that we would buy it, but Mr. Walker disappeared for (approximately) seven minutes when we asked to see fabric samples for a custom cover and matching throw pillows.

I don't think there was a shred of falsehood in our assumption that Mr. Split-log, proprietor of the Futons 'n' Things chain, did not instruct his employees to squander lucrative opportunities to sell accessories.

I remember giving Phoebe's shoulders a quick rub as I read the letter over her shoulder. "Ooh, that feels good," she said. "You're such a sweet guy. Feel like making coffee?"

The baby woke up while I was scooping grounds, and by the time I had settled her down and gotten the coffee started, Phoebe had finished a draft of the letter.

She asked me what I thought of the last part, which I figured would be where we asked for a discount or a free "fut-stool" or something, but instead we told Mr. Split-log that as proprietors of A&P Customer Service Consultants, LLC, we would like to discuss with him the possibility of contracting to assess customer service quality at all seven of his stores statewide.

"We don't have a customer service company," I objected.

"No, but we could," Phoebe said, with a smile.

I suppose that possessing an idea for a company of that name, which we would form the moment Mr. Split-log contacted us, did make us proprietors of it, in a sense.

Phoebe asked me to proofread the letter, and I suggested using 'distasteful' in place of 'obnoxious'. "Sweet *and* smart," she marveled. She played with fonts until the page had the look of corporate letterhead, then sent me out for some high-quality stationery.

When we laid down in bed that night, Phoebe nestled into the crook of my arm and gazed at the ceiling. "Just think," she said. "Our own company. If this pans out, I'll need some new suits and heels. You can't go to meetings with corporate types looking like someone who hangs out in sweats with a baby all day. I'd like a better cell phone, too."

"If we get other accounts and this thing really takes off, we could get a new car," I offered. I wasn't exactly lying, but I really didn't expect Mr. Split-log to take us up on our offer, much less expect to make a career out of customer service consulting. Sometimes you have to indulge people's fantasies, especially if you know how much they liked being mistaken for a lawyer back when they had worked for that law firm.

"If we do get the account, we're going to be totally professional about it. Good bookkeeping, the right clothes, businesslike words and gestures..."

"Ethics," I said.

She did a big nod. "Ethics. The whole bit." We studied the ceiling. I closed my eyes. "I'd love to rent an office downtown," she whispered. "In one of those old houses off the main drag? I can picture the sign out front, green with gold lettering: A&P Customer Service Consulting, LLC."

The phone rang early one morning. Phoebe picked it up. "A&P Customer Service Consulting, this is Phoebe," she said smoothly. "Oh, hi Mom. No, no — just practicing. It's hard to explain. So how are you?"

It rang again late that afternoon. Phoebe was in the bathroom. "A&P Customer Service Consulting!" she shouted, to remind me.

"Okay!" I yelled, and then picked up the phone. "A&PCSC."

"Alex?" said a gravelly voice.

"Speaking."

"Fred Split-log here. Just looking over your letter of October third. Like to take you up on it if the figures look good. What's your schedule like tomorrow?"

I don't mind telling you I thought about hanging up right then. "I'm tied up in meetings all day," I mused, not untruthfully, although most people would not call piano lessons 'meetings'. "But my partner, Phoebe, is free... in the afternoon," I said slowly, as if I were consulting a calendar even as I spoke.

We went back and forth for a few moments — exact time, exact location of the Futons 'n' Things corporate headquarters and of Fred's office. Before I had hung up, Phoebe was there at my side, holding a hand towel and looking up at me expectantly. "Was that… ?" she asked happily, and all I had to do was nod for her to put her hands on my shoulders and jump up and down, then bury her face in my chest.

"Two o' clock tomorrow," I said.

"Oh my God, I need an instrument. And what should I charge? Watch Sarah for a minute while I get online."

It took more than a minute. I took Sarah to Plantation for a blueberry muffin and a cup of milk, then drove around pointing out holiday lights while she goo-gooed in her car seat. "Thank you so much," Phoebe said when we got back two hours later. "You're so awesome. I got a *lot* done while you were gone. I'm totally ready for the meeting. Except I need to go out and get an outfit."

When Sarah finally fell asleep after dinner, I looked through the materials Phoebe had thrown together. Anyone else would have thought she had gotten a degree in marketing or business, or whatever field customer service consultants get degrees in. She had drawn up a 'Memorandum of Understanding' detailing the service A&PCSC, LLC would provide and the compensation with which Futons 'n' Things, Ltd would reciprocate. Her (our) 'instrument' was a ten-question telephone survey targeted to recent customers whose phone numbers would be taken during whatever transaction, large or small, they had engaged in. The survey began with a chunk of boilerplate along the lines of (if I recall correctly — this may be a poor approximation), "Good afternoon/evening, Mr./Ms. ________, my name is ________ and I'm calling on behalf of A&P Customer Service Consulting, LLC. This is not a sales call. It is my understanding that you recently made a purchase at Futons 'n' Things at their _____ location. Would you have a few minutes to complete a survey regarding the customer service you experienced at Futons 'n' Things?" The 'Memorandum of Understanding' specified that A&PCSC would conduct 100 surveys per week, which seemed reasonable at the time.

"You're so awesome for taking care of Sarah while I close this deal, doing the dishes and fixing meals and everything," Phoebe said at bedtime. "You are just the greatest guy."

I smiled, keeping my head at an 'aw-shucks' angle. "You're great," I said. "It's amazing the way you've put this deal together."

We started making calls on Monday, and it soon became obvious that A&PCSC, LLC would need some help. "Okay, all we have to do is make about fifteen calls a day," Phoebe told me. Sounded simple enough. But Fred had made what he said were standard stipulations: no early-morning calls. No dinnertime calls. No calls after nine p.m.

Phoebe made most of the calls, unless Sarah was taking her afternoon nap, in which case I helped her. I might make a call or two after dinner, if Sarah fell asleep during the first book I read to her.

We had a massive printout of customer information from Futons 'n' Things' seven Gulf Coast locations, basically a list of everyone who had purchased a bed or couch or fut-stool or pillow — anything, even a little replacement wing-nut — with a credit card during the past month. Simple enough, except that only about one or two out of ten customers wound up completing the survey. I could hear Phoebe making her first call in the next room while Sarah and I stacked blocks on the living room floor. "Good afternoon, Mr. Abanasrinivasan, my name is Phoebe and I'm calling — Mr. Abanasrinivasan? Hello?"

Dial.

"Good afternoon, Mr. Afton, my name is Phoebe and I'm calling on behalf of A&PC — excuse me? Yes, that's correct, but I'm not calling on behalf of the grocery — excuse me? Well, I'm not sure about that. But if I could just — yes, I'm sure their prices were quite good, Mr. Afton. Yes. Yes. Yes. But if I could just — Mr. Afton? I'm calling about Futons 'n' — all right, sir. Thank you for your time."

Sigh. Dial.

"Good afternoon, Mrs. Allen? Oh, she's not? What would be a convenient time to reach her? I see. I see. I'm sorry to hear that. I hope she recovers quickly. No, no message."

Dial.

"Good afternoon, Mrs. Alberts, my name is Phoebe and I'm calling on behalf of A&P Customer Service Consulting, LLC. This is not a sales call. It is my understanding that you recently made a purchase at Futons 'n' Things at their Slidell location. Would you have a few minutes to complete a survey regarding the customer service you experienced at Futons 'n' Things?

You would? Oh, wonderful! All right, let's see. First of all, let me confirm that you purchased a Foldaway Futstool on February third at the Slidell location? Okay, good. Now, first of all, on a scale of one to five, five being 'agree strongly,' one being 'disagree strongly,' and three being 'no opinion,' would you say that the store was clean and orderly when you arrived? Beg pardon? Yes, ma'am. Five means agree strongly, one means disagree strongly — that's right, any number from one to five. Take your time."

Good old Mrs. Alberts. She was the first one to finish the survey. It took an hour to find someone else, although Mr. Craft got to the third question before someone rang his doorbell and he had to hang up.

Sarah was a little fussy, so I held her and fixed dinner as best as I could with one hand. Phoebe stopped calling at six and staggered into the kitchen looking haggard. "We need a second phone line," she moaned. "And a babysitter." She waved two sheets of paper, where she had logged customers' names, times of call, purchases, and survey responses. "This is taking forever."

She thought of a better idea during dessert and picked up the phone. "Mom? I have a favor to ask." Peggy already knew the triumphant story of Fred Split-log and A&PCSC, LLC, and so before long Phoebe was saying, "It's not hard to do — you just call someone on the list, ask a few questions, write down their responses, and then call the next person. I just made the first two calls myself."

Peggy refused to accept payment for helping out, but Phoebe's friend Janet welcomed the ten dollars per completed survey. I don't know what made Phoebe think

Daniel would want to make calls for us, but I didn't say anything. I just listened while she told him the whole story, knowing he was patiently waiting instead of interrupting her to say there was no way a pulmonologist such as himself would stoop to making telemarketing survey calls. "Oh, I see," Phoebe said when it was finally his turn to talk. "Of course. I understand. Well, Alex says to call him the next time you want to play racquetball down at Foxy's." Which I hadn't said, but the assumption was not unreasonable.

I gave Phoebe permission to call my twin sisters up in Missouri. Julie consented, but Marya did not. By the time Phoebe finished explaining the process to Julie and promising to Fedex her part of the customer list the next day, it was time to go to bed. "A&PCSC, LLC is growing," Phoebe said happily. "We should have no trouble doing 100 surveys by Sunday night."

Janet called us the next day during dinner. "These people are morons," she told me. "Let me talk to Phoebe." Phoebe's mom didn't call until the next morning. I heard Phoebe telling her to keep trying. Julie called me around lunchtime. "I'm not getting anywhere," she said. "It's too much to say in too little time. Is it okay to call the company Applesauce? It takes a long time to say A&PCSC, LLC."

"If you think it'll help," I said, shrugging.

Sunday night rolled around much too quickly, and with half an hour to go Phoebe and I sat in the dining room, stacks of paper everywhere, dialing and talking like mad. Sarah had just gone to sleep and so I was on the cell phone, trying to get through to Ms. Cynthia Richard and then Mr. Alfred Robertson and Mr.

Clinton Robichaux. "We're not going to make it," Phoebe said at last. She leaned her head on one hand, staring a hole through the dining table. "It's nine oh three. We've only got eighty-seven surveys. Tomorrow's Monday. I have to give Fred Split-Log a complete report."

"Oh well," I said. "What else can we do?" I leaned back, relieved that the whole Applesauce fiasco was at an end.

She sat up straight, pushing her hair back behind her ears. "You're right," she said. "We don't really have a choice." She got into her typing posture, hands poised above the keyboard, eyes on the screen. "Hello, Ms. Richard," she said to herself, typing. "So you would give store cleanliness a four, and employee courtesy a three? All righty."

"You can't do this," I could have said, but I didn't. Instead I got up from the table and made for the kitchen as if I wanted something. Was that dishonest of me? Was it dishonest of me to smile half an hour later, when Phoebe came to the bedroom where I was reading and announced that she had finished? She sat at the end of the bed and mused that it was not so bad, really, that we just had to take a little shortcut in the first week. "Eighty-seven percent of the surveys are for real," she declared, and looked straight at me. I regret to inform you that I just shrugged and nodded, as if there were nothing wrong with a thirteen percent fabrication.

"I'm sure we'll get to one hundred percent next week," I said confidently.

"Oh, definitely," Phoebe said.

Phoebe met with Fred the next day to review the

results with his sales managers, and according to her it went very well. "He was impressed," she said, beaming. "He shook my hand before I left and said, 'I look forward to your next report, Ms. Chinstake.'" She did a pretty fair rendition of Fred's rough monotone, then added, "Do you think he has the hots for me?" with a laugh.

Janet reluctantly agreed to keep trying to make some calls. "Who else can we ask?" Phoebe wondered the next day, and called some guy she used to work with. She asked me to go talk to the neighbors, but I pretended to forget, because who wants to go talk to a retired couple you hardly know about making a little extra money they probably don't need by engaging in some obscure, frustrating pursuit? "How about that guy you played racquetball with a few times?" she asked.

"That contractor? I guess I could try to find his number." I shrugged, knowing I would do no such thing. I could hardly imagine how the conversation would go. *Hi, Rob? Yeah, this is Alex. I don't know if you remember — we met at Foxy's a few months ago, played racquetball a few times. Piano teacher, right. Yeah, glasses. That's me. Listen, I need you to call a bunch of far-flung senior citizens, busy housewives, and unreliable college students and ask them some questions they won't care about. I'll pay you ten dollars per survey, which'll probably work out to about a dollar an hour, judging from the way things have been going.*

Phoebe did convince her cousin Rita, whom we had last seen at the baby shower, to make some calls before and after her shift at the nursing home, and one of her mom's friends agreed to give it a shot, though she had so many questions about how to do it that it wound up taking up a lot of Phoebe's time. I learned to look and sound busy any time the phone rang.

We made calls every chance we got. Sarah's naps got longer, her bedtime earlier. We ate frozen dinners and drank from plastic cups. I think we started talking too fast, having to remind ourselves that someone picking up the phone in Shreveport will need a minute to process *HelloMrsGibsonmynameisAlexandI'mcalling onbehalfofApplesauce. Thisisnotasalescall. Itismyunder standingthatyourecentlymadeapurchaseatFutons'n'Things. Canyoudoasurveyaboutit?*

A few of those F 'n' T customers got wily, some pretending their phones were malfunctioning — *What? Is anyone there? I can't hear you!* — some telling outright lies — *I've never been to Futons 'n' Whatchacallit; you must be mistaken* — and some getting downright smart-alecky — *My wife hit me on the head with a frying pan last night and I have amnesia* or *Who's Mr. Trenton? This is Britney Spears.*

"Twenty-four percent," Phoebe sighed when it was all over on Sunday night. I was already in bed, because it takes quite a while to whip up twenty-four fake surveys that don't all sound alike.

"We've got to do better," I told her.

"I know." Phoebe frowned. "We will. We're still getting Applesauce set up and organized. Maybe if we went ahead and leased some office space."

She was pretty frantic the next morning, rushing around looking for the right shoes and cussing herself out for not having bought at least one more good outfit. Sarah cried and cried when Phoebe left, but I let her slap at the keys while I played lullabies on the piano with one hand, which made her happy.

Phoebe danced through the door two hours later. "Look what I've got," she sang, waving a pale green envelope. Sarah reached for it, but Phoebe kept it out of her reach. "Applesauce is making money now," she said, kissing the baby.

She convinced me that we had time to go to lunch before my first student of a full afternoon showed up. "He'll wait for you if we're a little late," she said. I played along all through lunch, agreeing with Phoebe's speculations that she could run to the mall before dinner to pick up a nice suit and it would be a good idea to look through the classifieds for office space and a not-too-old used car might be within reach now and I too had always wanted a secretary working for me and a magnetic sign for the car, with the company name, phone number, and web address, would probably not cost much.

Fred left us a message while Phoebe was on the phone, I was teaching, and Sarah was napping. Phoebe made me listen to it. "Need to talk to y'all about quality control," was about all he said.

"You see?" Phoebe said deliriously. "He wants us to expand the contract. Maybe he'll give us some office space at F 'n' T headquarters."

"He sounds mad," I said.

She just laughed. "He always sounds like that. He's just gruff. Gruff gruff gruff! Like an old St. Bernard or something."

I don't know what I was thinking on Tuesday afternoon when the phone rang while I was between calls and Phoebe was dealing with a nasty diaper, because lately most of our calls had been Rita or what's-her-face asking lame questions or just complaining about not being able to complete surveys, but I answered it. "Applesauce," I said.

"Alex?" said a gruff voice, more like a grizzly bear than a St. Bernard.

"Speaking. Mr. Split-log?"

"We have a problem," he said. "My store manager in Monroe was on the customer list, and I have here a completed survey in his name, but he tells me that no one ever called him. Can you explain how that could happen?"

"Sir, I — you have to understand, sir," I began, with no idea of what I would say next. By now Phoebe was back, holding Sarah and studying my face with an expectant smile. "We have some new employees," I said. "And we have already seen some evidence that one of them is not especially reliable. My guess would be that this individual may be responsible for the situation. If you could provide the name of the customer, I will check our records and take appropriate action."

"I won't stand for this sort of thing," Fred growled.

"Neither will we, sir, neither will we. I can guarantee you that it will not happen again." By now Phoebe was cramming her eyebrows together, raising furrows all along her forehead.

Fred cleared his throat, now sounding like a grizzly with a splintered bone caught in its throat. "Just so we're clear: did you or Phoebe knowingly falsify or allow falsifying of surveys?"

I wanted to hand the phone to Phoebe right then and

let her pick up the pieces herself. But I didn't. Instead, I lied. "No sir, we did not."

"All right then. I'd like to meet with either you or Phoebe about some sort of quality assurances for these surveys, some sort of verification or spot-check system."

"We'd be happy to do that."

"What the hell?" Phoebe asked after I had hung up.

"No more fake surveys," I said. I felt flushed. "You did a fake survey on one of his store managers, and Fred found out about it."

"Oh my God."

"He sounded pretty steamed."

"Oh my God."

"Do we even know what the hell we're doing?"

"We do, we do," Phoebe said. Sarah started crying. "It just takes a while to get situated."

"I say we cancel this contract, apologize, return the money. We're way over our heads here."

"All right, Alex," she said. "All right."

The house was quiet for the rest of the day. No constant telephony. For dinner I made a pretty fair étouffée with some crawfish tails I had picked up at Piggly Wiggly. Sarah seemed happier, too, cooing and giggling the way she used to. She went right to bed after supper, and I got in a good two hours' practice with the keyboard and headphones. Phoebe was reading in bed when I came into the bedroom to change into my pajamas. She watched me for a while, and I gave her a reluctant half-smile.

"I've been thinking," she said. "What do you say we just finish out the week? I mean, all of the calling we did yesterday and today would just go to waste if we didn't. Plus, who knows? I feel like we're about to get it together, like this time Applesauce can get the fakeness down to zero percent. If we quit now, Fred'll take that as an admission of guilt."

I sighed with clenched lips, shaking my head.

"Come on. Just five more days."

"And then that's it," I said. "No more after that."

"Oh, definitely. Yeah, no way."

The whole time I was brushing my teeth I was thinking that I knew Phoebe well enough by now that I could see where this was going. She'd drop hints here and there the rest of the week, then Sunday night talk me into going one more week, then one more month, and on and on. I may have spat out the toothpaste more loudly than usual.

"You were awesome on the phone," Phoebe said after I had gotten into bed. "Fred was like putty in your hands. I could tell. And you used words that he loves, words like 'individual' and 'situation.'"

I gave a vague grunt, shrugging.

"And then that étouffée you made! It was amazing. You're so good."

"Yeah, compared to you," I said, and I didn't mutter it. No, I said it clear as day, because how honest is it to say something if the other person can't hear it?

Phoebe just laughed as if she thought I was joking. Then she yawned, snuggled down into the pillow, and closed her eyes.

nature of theft:

Dear Alicia and Dustin:

You're divorced now, but you have to admit that the tale of your formation of a customer service consulting company makes good TV. I suppose you have many reasons for indignation — I stole your lives, of course, but then I had the gall to change the electronics store to a futon store, alter your hair colors and professions, and do other fiddling things that imply that although your lives are interesting, they are not quite interesting enough. A wise person (perhaps an advice columnist) once pointed out that it is easier to ask forgiveness than permission, which is why this is the first you've heard of "Applesauce."

down on luck

lindsay bower

A man come in the other day, to the restaurant where I work, and asked if I'd ever thought about getting a real job. I said no, sir — 'cause you always have to call men in suits and ties 'sir' — this one suits me fine. And he asked if I had kids, and I said no, sir. And he asked then why I wasn't going to college, so I said, 'cause I don't want to, sir, I like my job, and then he said you should look into college. So I said, but who else's gonna do my job if I don't? You? And he laughed and tipped me five extra dollars, and told me to go buy a lottery ticket, 'cause I deserved to live somewhere where it was sunny all the time. So then I told him I don't get lottery tickets at all no more, not since the day I thought I won when I didn't, 'cause that was like love for me, that day, I doubt it'd happen but once in a lifetime, and thanks, but that day was enough heartache for me. So he said, woman, save up, get you some nickels and go to Vegas, you look like the kind of person that needs

Vegas — Vegas always smiles on a beautiful woman. And I said that would be nice, you know, everybody having the time of their lives, nothing but good luck, and yeah, the world would be better, but it's a hard thing believing it could happen for real. I told him I'd look Vegas up on a map and see how far away it is, and I did that night, and Vegas is 2,345 miles away. I never been on a plane, but I know nickels don't buy nobody a plane ticket, and by the time I save my nickels, Vegas won't smile on an eighty year old.

There were a whole lot of blackbirds, I remember, sitting on the telephone line across the street. That's the first thing I remember seeing that day, waking up and looking out and seeing all them just sitting there, then up they flew, scattering away like ants when a foot scrapes away an anthill. Mama was already gone for a double at Texas Roadhouse, having to leave early to fill up the gas tank on her way. The Chevy leaked gas like a faucet. There were birds and the world for me, just for me, for eight hours. Eight whole hours. No school, nothing. The gray outside made me not want to go to school, but it wasn't like I liked to go to school when it was sunny either. I used to get pissed off seeing the other girls put lip gloss on all the time, in front of the mirror in the bathroom, at their desks, at lunch, all the damn time, every thirty minutes like some asshole make-up timer went off.

I'd started wearing lip gloss a while back though, 'cause tomboys always come around, and it's what teenage girls do, think they ought to be like every other teenage girl. I bought some from Wal-Mart, this clear, gloopy, glittery crap that made my lips sticky and my hair get caught on my mouth when the wind blew. My friend Chris — she was a girl — said we had to put our lip gloss on at the same time when we was at school, 'cause boys'd like it. So we'd slick it on whenever we was in the hall and talking, but not talking really, just looking around to see who was looking at us, and a black boy at school had asked me for my phone number the day before the gray day when I was alone.

He'd asked for my number, and said I was thick. I'd guessed it was a good thing, being thick; you wouldn't ask somebody for a phone number if it was bad. His name was Trémon and he wrote a little dash above the 'e', 'cause I looked when he turned his papers in. I'd heard he had a girlfriend named Jasmine that wore Nikes and tennis skirts, sometimes knee socks, and she was popular, so I wondered why he wasn't calling her. Maybe they'd broken up. I wished I'd had Trémon's phone number, in case he'd skipped school too, and I'd have asked him to come over, 'cause I had nothing to lose and no one to hang out with. *My parents ain't home. So come on over. Let's have some fun.* It's what other girls did. I wanted us to get drunk on the Malibu and Jim Beam in the cabinet.

On the gray day I was pretty much stuck, and I'd told myself I'd do something I couldn't ever do when I was in school. Nothing bad, like breaking in somewhere or doing graffiti or knocking over mailboxes, just something I couldn't do 'cause I was in school. And I'd decided on a lottery ticket, to buy one from the convenient store near the front of Royal Pines, where we lived, the convenient store that was a gas station too. Most people in Royal Pines went to the convenient store when there was nothing to do, and they stood out front, black guys and white guys that wanted to be black guys, waiting. They'd wait, and they'd chew tobacco, and they'd smoke blunts, and they'd drink blue bulls out of brown paper bags, and sometimes they'd spit their brown sludge on the cars getting gas.

My brother Dogleg, he was seven, had got caught stealing my daddy's chewing tobacco the day before. He'd taken it on the bus for his friends and got in trouble at school when the bus driver took a quick right turn, and the pack spilled its brown shreds all over the floor. We'd all called him Dogleg since he was two, 'cause before he could walk he'd run on all fours, leg and arm, then leg and arm, just like a dog. It's hard telling people about it, 'cause it was something you had to see to know why he was called Dogleg. But his real name's Corey.

He'd get the bus at six in the morning, even though school was only a few blocks away. He liked riding around with his friends, going through all the neighborhoods. They'd throw their half-eaten Pop Tarts and empty Coke bottles out the bus windows and onto the lawns of the houses in the nice neighborhoods. When they'd come home, the bus stopped outside the convenient store — 'cause the bus don't ever take kids to the front doors of trailers — and they'd all spit when they got off, my brother and his friends. One by one, they'd all step down, spitting to the left or right, but always spitting; seven years old with clean and clear spit trying to be like the bad-ass dropouts that stood out front the Save-a-Lot.

That was the name of the convenient store, but

nobody called it that, probably 'cause it sounded stupid, like you was excited about saving money. Nobody really shopped there, just went there, like me, getting dressed that morning like I was going somewhere, like I was going to school maybe, even though I knew I wasn't. I'd put my shoes on, white Reeboks I bought with money from working at Kroger. Sometimes we said we worked at the K-Roger and the guys in the meat department would say who's Roger and we would all laugh, even though they always said it and we always laughed. I only worked at the K-Roger two days a week, before school for two hours, after school for two hours. I'd saved up for a month before I could buy those Reeboks.

It was something I never did, buy lottery tickets, 'cause I was never home for the Final Draw, and that was the only one that mattered, the Final Draw, and you had to be 18 to buy a ticket too, though nobody ever said nothing if you wasn't and wanted to buy one. In the Final Draw they drew the five numbers, you picked your numbers first, and then you saw if what you picked matched up with the numbers on TV. It wasn't just scratching at a ticket with a quarter, scratching away your luck, 'cause you'd probably only ever win five dollars. It was the only one you had a say in, the only one that made sense, the only one worth spending a dollar on. *Spend a dollar, get yourself a million.*

I remember Royal Pines as I walked down the hill, how quiet it was during the day, most kids in school like I was supposed to be, or hiding 'cause they wasn't, and most adults at work. I remember thinking I maybe should have locked the door to the trailer; no matter, my parents never did either, and my mama always said put your fortune in the hands of the Lord. It ain't like there was much to steal inside anyway, except food and maybe one of my daddy's guns. He never kept any bullets though.

It was quiet the whole walk down, and I didn't see one soul, except a lady out front watering some plants hanging from the ceiling of her kinda front porch. They did that, lots of the old people in Royal Pines, made themselves a porch, and we called the porches kinda front porches, 'cause they wasn't really. They'd put down green turf you could buy by the yard at Vick's Hardware in Elgin, then add some plastic chairs, put up an awning off the side of the trailer, and overnight, there'd be a porch, and what looked like a new trailer. My daddy always said he'd be damned if he ever did that, 'cause the last thing he wanted to do was spend time outside the trailer looking at a bunch of other trailers.

When I got to the convenient store, there was a boy that looked like Trémon standing outside eating a honey bun, and he called me over to him, but I acted like I didn't hear. I went inside and thought about getting a pack of cigarettes 'cause none of the people working at the convenient store ever checked ID, even though they all knew you wasn't 18 or 21, so I went straight up to the cashier.

"Can I get a pack of Reds? And a Final Draw," I said.

"Just one?"

I had a dollar left over.

"Give me two tickets. I'll fill out two."

She handed me two tickets and one of those little yellow pencils with no eraser.

"You got ID?" she asked, with her back to me, already rooting around for the pack of Reds.

"No. I'm 18."

She turned around and looked at me like she wasn't about to give me the Reds.

"Bring it next time or I ain't selling you no more packs. We had cops come in here last week and I 'bout lost my job."

I gave her five dollars and told her I didn't want the pennies. I remember scrunching up my eyes and trying hard to concentrate on the tickets, looking down at all the numbers, a gazillion different things you could pick — only the right ones that would set you free. I remember picking 43, 'cause that was how old Mama was, then 52, 'cause that was how old Daddy was, then 7, for Dogleg, and 16, for me. The last number I picked was 6: T-R-É-M-O-N.

For the second ticket I looked around the convenient store, looked for a sign, something, anything — a machine called Tiffany's Cafe. I took my tickets and went over, saw it sold cappuccinos, mochaccinos, espressos, hot chocolate, chicken soup. Five things — I circled a 5. Everything was 97 cents. Seven letters in Tiffany. I was 16. And 6 for Trémon, again, 'cause he was on my mind — that's how it is when a boy asks a girl for her number and the girl's never had a boy ask for her number. 5, 97, 7, 16, 6. I remember feeling like I was holding gold right there in my hand.

I gave her the tickets and I remember wondering how they got the numbers from your ticket to whoever was in charge of the lottery. She punched some things into a machine and printed me out two receipts with my numbers.

"They're for you to keep. So you know if you win or not," she said.

I thanked her and walked off, shoving the pack of Reds into my jeans pocket, a bell over the door jingling when I opened it to leave.

"Pssst. Girl, I saw you got cigs. Give me one."

I looked at him this time and he looked alright, so I thought what the hell, we'll both smoke one, and reached into my pocket, took them out, started hitting the pack against my hand, like everybody did.

"What's your name?"

"Tiffany."

I took the plastic wrap off and unfolded the foil, brought one cigarette out and handed it to him.

"You go to L.E. Wry Middle?"

"I'm sixteen," I said. "I go to high school."

He pulled a lighter out of his pocket and lit up, handed me it when he was done.

"Do you know Trémon?" I asked.

"No. Does he got a brother?"

"No. I'm his girlfriend. The one he dumped Jasmine for."

He laughed and blew smoke out his nostrils.

"You could be my girlfriend," he said, taking a puff.

"My parents ain't home. We could hang out. There's Malibu."

"Where you live?"

I pointed up the hill, into Royal Pines. He nodded and we both started walking, taking in smoke and breathing it out through our nostrils.

"I bought tickets for the Final Draw. Spend a dollar,

get yourself a million."

He laughed again and told me to call him AK, and I asked him what AK stood for and he said AK-47. I said there wasn't no way I was calling him AK-47, so he best give up a name, and he said his name was Andre. I remember the lady still watering her plants and I remember wondering if Trémon might get mad, seeing us walking together, and then hoping Trémon would see us walking together, and get mad. First thing I thought about buying, I remember, was a car, so there'd be no more walking, and it would have been the best thing to ride up that hill with the windows down and some music all loud, whatever music Andre wanted to play.

"What you got to drink?" Andre asked, and he'd taken four of my Reds on the walk home, and was on his fifth, sitting at the table in our kitchen.

"Malibu. Jim Beam. Coke."

"Get the 'Bu and Beam. Fuck the Coke."

Andre didn't smile, but he laughed in this way, I remember, that made me feel like he was stealing things from me, like he was getting away with taking things right there, right as I was watching him.

"You got anything else? Bacardi? Hennessy?"

I looked in the cabinet under the TV, looked all the way in the back, nothing. Second thing I thought about buying, I remember, was a cabinet full of liquor.

I shook my head, coming up with the two bottles. I walked back over to the kitchen table and set them down, reached into another cabinet to get two mugs.

One was my Daddy's that had a woman in a bikini on it and when the mug got hot, her bikini disappeared. The other mug was one from the Bob and Tom show on K97, a big cartoon of Bob and Tom on it, carrying fishing poles. I didn't think about shot glasses then, like I guess I would now, 'cause when you're sixteen it don't matter what you're drinking from or what you're drinking, though I don't guess I'd mind all that much now either.

I poured us a mugful each of Malibu, took the mug with the bikini woman on it, and handed Bob and Tom to Andre.

"You don't talk much," I said.

Andre just looked at me and took a sip from the mug, laid his cigarette down in my Daddy's ashtray.

"How old are you?" I asked.

"Twenty."

"You don't look twenty. You look about sixteen. Like me," I said.

"I'm sixteen then."

We both took sips of Malibu, puffed on our cigarettes at the same time. I remember it was like dancing, the two of us. I'd take a sip, then he did, then we both did, then we'd both end with a puff. And we sat there like that for about twenty minutes, not saying much. I'd take a sip, then he did, then we both did, then we'd both end with a puff.

"When your parents coming home?" Andre asked. "Your daddy might get a shotgun on AK."

"My daddy works late. And Mama's working a double. And my brother don't come home till after school. Four o' clock or so."

I took a puff, looked down at the pack, thought we might be getting toward the end, and sure enough, only two was left.

"Give me some money for some more cigs. I'll go get a pack," said Andre.

"I don't got any money. I'll look for some later. Let's drink. My mama and daddy play drinking Monopoly. We could play drinking Monopoly."

He didn't say nothing.

"I'll get it out," I said, and went to the cupboard where the game was before he could say no, or make me feel like a dumbass for saying we should do something more than just sit there.

I got the box out, the box with the edges broken and bits torn off from when we had a dog, the dog that got run over when he wandered out toward the convenient store and the main road. When I took the top off, all the stuff inside was a big mess, 'cause like I said, Mama and Daddy used to play drinking Monopoly, so when it was done, there wasn't much time for cleaning up. I got out a few pieces, laid them on the table, an iron and a car, and there wasn't but two more pieces left, when there should have been a handful — but Mama and Daddy had lost the rest of the pieces over the years.

"You know how to play Monopoly? You roll the dice, then you either buy the property you land on or you don't. You make yourself a millionaire. Or you might go to jail."

"What about drinking?" asked Andre, and I remember he looked like he was about done with me, done with the no cigarettes, done with just the Malibu, done with the Monopoly.

"If you don't buy the property you land on, you know, if you don't got enough money to buy it, you drink. You always end up having to drink. And when we're done and drunk, it'll be time for Final Draw and you can watch me win and we'll have a party."

Andre laughed and reached for the last cigarette. I'd decided already he could have both cigarettes, shoved the pack at him so he'd know I didn't want another one.

"You know there ain't but one person in a damn blue moon that wins that thing? And you ain't even eighteen, so you can't get the money anyway," said Andre, and it was about the most he'd said all day, the whole time I'd known him, and it was like he was trying to bring me down or something, when I knew I was going to win and he was just jealous, thinking I wasn't going to give him any.

"I'll give you a house if I win," I said. "And your friends. I'll give them houses and cars too."

"You ain't gonna have any money left after that."

"I'll have enough to buy myself an island to go live on. And you can come with me if you want."

"Black folks don't like the sun."

"Suit yourself," I said, and he was an idiot for not wanting to be on an island, so he was better off staying here in a house I'd bought him.

"Now roll. You go first," I said, gave him the dice and waited.

He rolled and didn't say nothing, moved the horse to one of the purple squares — Baltic Avenue.

"I don't want to buy it," he said. "Do I still got to drink?"

"Yeah."

He drank the rest of the Malibu in his cup, took him only a few seconds and a few swallows.

I rolled and landed on a railroad property, knew there was no point in buying a railroad.

"Drink the rest," said Andre. "Like I did."

I opened my throat, downed the Malibu in a few swallows just like him, then almost puked it right back up, it was so damn sweet. I remember already feeling fuzzy and looking around and seeing everything in a blur and chewing on my lips so I could feel how I couldn't feel them.

We went a few more turns and Andre almost made it all the way around, but landed on jail, said he wasn't going to jail and threw his horse across the room.

I remember knowing why Mama and Daddy never cleaned up the Monopoly game like they should have, remember feeling like there was no point in doing a thing, feeling like I should be saving my energy for Final Draw that was coming up in ten minutes.

"Give me some of that Beam," Andre said, so I went over to the counter and opened it, thought about what I would do with the empty Malibu bottle, 'cause it had been half full and now we'd drunk it all, and Mama and Daddy would know I'd done it, but I poured us each a cup of the Beam.

Andre said we should play his game, his game that went like this — one, two, three, drink it all, no matter why or when or what — do it, now — one, two, three, and we both drank. Now after that, I was gone, maybe gone like I'd never been before, 'cause I'd never drank that much — except for stealing a few beers — 'cause I always thought I might get caught. I remember looking at the clock, knowing I'd already missed the start of the show and I needed to get to the TV right then as fast as I could or I'd miss out.

Andre was laughing and going on about something, so I told him to shut up, and ran to the television, pulled the lottery receipts out of my pocket and stared down, the letters foggy and fuzzy, scrunching my eyes together to see.

I remember the blonde lady coming on the screen — and her green sparkly dress — and she was at this machine, this machine where balls were flying around inside, then she pressed a button and up popped one of the balls, and she turned it around to face the camera.

Andre was still talking to himself about nothing and I told him to shut up again if he wanted me to buy him a house. The blonde lady turned the first ball around, and at first I remember thinking it was 48, but then I saw it was a 43, and knew then and there I'd have to make a list of things to buy tonight, that's what I'd be spending my night doing, 'cause I was the winner.

There'd be nothing to tell if the next number wasn't a 52, and it was, and the next number was 7, but I was so gone that I had to get right up to the TV and look at it, my nose almost touching the screen. I was so sure I was the winner and then she turned the fourth ball around and it was a 5, and for a second my heart did a leap, 'cause I knew that number, I'd circled that number, I'd picked that number, and I'd barely had time to think about what it all was before she'd turned the fifth ball around and I saw it was a 97.

"Those are my numbers!" I screamed, and I was

looking at my tickets and back up at the TV and back down at my tickets and back up at the TV.

"Let me see," said Andre, and I remember him getting up, coming over to where I was, and him almost looking white, even though he was black, like he'd seen a ghost. He grabbed the tickets from me and looked down and back up at the TV and back down at my tickets.

"It don't work like that," said Andre, and I knew what he meant, all of a sudden, and of course it didn't work like that, you was only supposed to buy one ticket and one set of numbers, not two sets and get half the numbers. Half don't get you nowhere.

"Give me some money for cigs," said Andre, and looked down at me still sitting there in front of the TV.

I remember not saying a thing, in shock 'cause I was so close, and so I told him to shut up and go away, I didn't have no more money.

"Man, fuck you then," he said, threw my receipts at me and walked toward the door, then came back, took the Beam on the counter and ran out.

I didn't care about the Beam, but thought about what I would tell my mama and daddy, and then supposed if we'd drank it I'd still be in the same boat. I looked down at the receipts and picked them up, looked at them, and looked at the TV, the blonde woman talking about how last week's winner was Dale Marsh, a trucker from Pineville, how he'd retired and now drove a Mercedes.

I could have done something big, like tear the receipts in half and scream, or burn them, or flush them down the toilet, spit on them as they was going down, but I just crumpled them up and threw them in the trash, on top of the empty Malibu bottle and my Daddy's empty beer cans, on top of the broken egg shells from when Mama made him breakfast before he went to work the day before.

I went outside and stood on the steps, saw some kids getting home from school, and I knew my brother would be getting home soon. It was sunny and I was still pretty gone, but it was nice, being outside, and I wasn't thinking about the Final Draw, but knew I needed to clean up some before Dogleg got back or he'd cry 'cause it smelled like booze. He always cried when it smelled like booze 'cause he knew he wouldn't get to sleep in Mama and Daddy's bed.

I stayed home from school for three more days, told my parents I was sorry. They believed me, let me get away with the drinking 'cause I'd never done a thing like that before, play hooky and get drunk, though I remember thinking it sure wouldn't be the last time. I stayed home from school for three more days and bought a ticket for the Final Draw each day, and a pack of Reds. I remember I sat, alone and smoking, and dreamed up what I'd buy, alone 'cause I made sure there wasn't an Andre or a Trémon to take away all my attention. I still think maybe that's what happened, and maybe it was them that was bad luck — boys, I thought, who'd make it all better, but just brought me down. I lost interest after those three days, staying home, and went back to school, realized nobody'd let a sixteen year old win the Final Draw anyway, even if I did. Andre was right. So I went back to school for a while, but then Trémon dropped out later on that year, and so did I — about a year after that — but it's not like we dropped out 'cause of each other or nothing. He never called, and I never saw him after he dropped out, so maybe he's got pretty babies with Jasmine now.

So when this man come into work the other day, like I said, I told him no thanks, no thanks about the lottery and Vegas and all that. I try to keep away from all that nonsense, though we got this video poker machine now in the restaurant toward the front, and it's real popular, even though there's all this arguing going around about whether it's good or not. People keep saying we ought to take the machines out of a family restaurant, and the gas stations ought to take theirs out too, 'cause it all just supports gambling and drinking.

I seen it, the men they're talking about, the ones that bring their paychecks and sit for hours at the video poker machine and get drunk, then go home and pass out. At least they ain't beating on their wives. I seen them, sitting there, most enjoying beers and Reds, and I could see why you'd want to play on those machines, even if you just spend five minutes after work taking your chances. It's easier than buying tickets and all that, with video poker, 'cause it's just poker, and you can win five dollars, easy, so I'm sure it's nice, having five extra dollars and hoping more might come if you just play long enough.

nature of theft:

When I was 13, I moved to South Carolina, and it was quite an adjustment for a child who had never traveled to the Southern United States. I had a difficult time making friends, and the first good friend I did make was a girl I probably would have never made friends with back home — we were from completely different backgrounds. My parents were very well educated and artistic, and her parents were blue-collar, superstitiously religious, and hardly ever home. One of the first things I remember her telling me the day we made friends, is the day before, she'd skipped school and bought a lottery ticket. I was in complete awe, but I remember thinking what a contrast her chosen way to spend a skipped day of school was to what mine would have been; I'm sure I would have spent all day reading. I don't know what she's doing now, or if she did drop out of school (she was definitely headed in that direction), because after I found my feet in South Carolina, and found more friends, we drifted apart. I suppose this story qualifies as 'stolen' because I stole the circumstances from her, filled the rest in with my imagination, and ended up with my own interpretation of what it all meant in the grand scheme of things.

not dead yet, lily?

ron butlin

With the approach of the thunderstorm Lily was growing more and more restless. As the air became clammier and heavier, every breath stuck in her lungs like sweat. Outside, the sky had darkened to blue-black. The window was open but no draught came in. Four in the afternoon, midsummer almost, and dark enough indoors to have to switch on the light. But she wouldn't.

Instead, having struggled to her feet, she stood in the airless front room listening to herself gasp for breath — she'd better wait a moment before setting off to the kitchen for a drink of water. She didn't want to have the likes of Mrs MacDonald come in to find her keeled over at last. Sometimes it felt as if the whole street was waiting for her to go. All these neighbourly visits about nothing in particular, except to check she'd not died in her sleep. They were being kind, and she supposed she was grateful, but there was always the unspoken pause, the split-second's refocusing of a glance that betrayed the real question:

Not dead yet?

Well, she appreciated their concern, but fuck them.

Yes, that was the only language to use. In the last few weeks Lily had discovered the relish of bad language. One morning she'd been woken by Mrs Miller phoning to ask, after the 'not-dead-yet?' pause, if she wanted something from the shop. She'd said no, then hung up.

Now for breakfast, she'd thought, breakfast, bloody breakfast. As she pulled on her dressing-gown she'd started muttering to herself:

"Bloody breakfast, bloody, bloody, bloody, bloody breakfast."

It felt good, stimulating. Like a vigorous marching tune in her head. There she stood in front of the mirror: a kindly-looking, white-haired, elderly woman, frail but dignified — those were no doubt the sort of words her neighbours used when talking about her — and all the time behind the benevolent smile she was hammering out full-force, "BLOODY, BLOODY, BLOODY, BLOODY breakfast." Then she'd grinned to herself — and she'd not done that in months.

In a short time the 'bloodies' had given way to 'hells', and the 'hells' to 'damns' — but getting into 'fucks' had been her big breakthrough. It was after the postman went by a couple of days ago: *No letters, well fuck him!* she'd thought, then announced,

"Fuck him! Fuck him! Fuck him!" to the clock, the empty armchair and a whole clutch of wedding photographs. Stopping herself in time from getting too loud. Not because it might shock the MacDonalds and Millers or whoever might be passing. She didn't care about them; it was simply because she didn't really want to share these words with anyone: they were hers, and hers alone.

But her words weren't working today. "Fucking storm, fucking storm," she kept repeating as she stood in the kitchen letting the tap run for coolness, but didn't feel any better. The water tasted heavy and tepid. She'd go into the garden.

The sky was much blacker than before with everything beneath gripped in sharp, shadowless light, and the air so sluggish she almost had to push her way through it. Nothing seemed to move out there. Across the street she could see the MacDonalds, a group of stuffed figures crouched in a family circle around their patio table. Who were the MacDonalds, who were the Millers? Where had they come from? Where had any of the people in the street come from with their tracksuits, their baggy shorts, their baseball caps, their mobile phones and their internets?

The heaviness in the air seemed to have turned that bush by her front gate completely rigid. When she gave one of the branches a tug, it shook — she could tell — unwillingly. Her neighbour's brand-new spade was propped just within reach; without thinking what she was doing, she picked it up. Its metal edge clanged against the stone path, a *clang* that seemed to fill the street. Too bad. She clanged it once more and her reward was five MacDonald faces panned in her direction.

As she leant towards the bush its perfume stuck to her skin and, in its sultriness, the scent seemed almost a solid thing. Perhaps, the air being so still, if she removed the plant and its scent, she could fit herself into the gap left behind, and so withdraw from a world filled with strangers bringing their strange ways.

She started spading out earth. Not so hard really, but with every thrust and lift she had to stop to catch her breath. There was sweat trickling down her face and back. She paused for a moment to wipe her eyes clear — and *there*, up on their hind legs, were a couple of MacDonalds staring over at her. The bigger of them, a wobble of pink flesh, baldness and glasses, was already starting in her direction.

She carried on digging. Not that she could remember what the plant was called, nor what anything much was called these days, only that some things were alive and some things weren't. Really, who cared? One good tug and she'd have it free.

The wobbly MacDonald was standing at her gate: "Mrs Williams! Hello there, Mrs Williams!"

Should she pretend to have gone deaf?

Yes.

Taking a good grip of the stem with both hands, feet braced for the effort, she closed her eyes for the Big Tug.

"Hello there, Mrs Williams! That's a lovely lilac you've got there. Can I help you at all?"

The bush came out more easily than she'd expected, almost first pull, making her stagger a couple of steps backwards. She threw it to one side then picked up the spade again.

"You really should be resting in weather like this, Mrs Williams. What are you doing?"

Before she could stop herself she'd replied, "Digging my fucking grave. At my age what the fuck else would I be doing?"

When she next looked up the MacDonald had gone.

Indoors, it was almost dark. She went through to the kitchen to wash her hands, then sat down as the first rumble of thunder sounded. Heavy drops of rain began spattering the window. Feeling a bit tired after all that digging, she might just have a short nap now — while she was in the mood.

nature of theft:

My wife and I were visiting her parents. It was a hot-hot day with a thunderstorm threatening. Out of the house opposite came a very elderly lady carrying a pickaxe.

Regi's parents told me this woman had always been the model of convention — it seemed that for most of her life she never did anything wrong, never said anything wrong. Always the prim and proper lady. Until, that is, she turned eighty. Then something must have happened. No one quite knows what — and for the last five years she's been doing exactly what she pleases, when and how she pleases. She's taken up drinking whisky, and has stopped going to church.

As I sat in my parents-in-laws' garden I watched the elderly woman attack the bush with her pickaxe. The thunder boomed — and she carried on pickaxing. The rain started — we went indoors, but not the old lady. She remained out there while the storm raged around her. Finally, having removed the offending laurel, she returned indoors.

a tree guards the road

lucille valentine

I thought I had overslept, thought with a panicked heart, sweaty upper lip that it was mid-morning, by which time the sun falls full in by my bedroom window. I was by the door in one movement and past the unsteady walls in another. I could smell burned toast. When I reached the kitchen with my hair trailing somewhere behind, they were only having breakfast — Dad, Mom and Max. Dad was already in his uniform but Mom still in a gown. As I fumbled at my chair, I bumped my plate onto the floor. The stupid old thing broke and Dad leaned forward out of his chair and slapped me, told me to catch a wakeup. Or else. Mom snatched my shoulder, "Clean up the mess," she said. She felt my burning arm, then my cheek with her palm, and then my forehead. It was back to bed for me. She tested my burning dragon mouth with a flick, flick thermometer. I had a fever and a coated tongue and had to miss school, which was a pity.

Dreaming of swimming in a sea of lava, I felt softer, puffed-out bread dough and crisped on the outside. A bath was filled, the water at room temperature to cool me, and like the room, it was sun-warmed, borehole water that lay down a red sediment and came from an underground lake, kept filled by the Okavango, my dad said. I floated in the water, the earth, the soothing balm, until I saw Mita's legs by my side; her blue-and-white check housecoat parted below the last button showing her kind, worn knees and dark brown calves. She had brought me sweet rooibos tea though I could also taste something else — some bush herbs maybe — and she brought me baby biscuits, Marie biscuits. I slept again and bathed again and slept again until the prrrrrrr of the plane bringing Rebecca and the other children back from the interschool athletics roused me. I pulled on a dress.

Supper for the children was always early in our house, and I joined Max at the table, walking past Mita washing the bath. With my thighs sticking to the green melamine chair I forked cooked potato in fatty mutton gravy around my plate making a slow inward spiral. My elegant mother leaned on the windowsill; she was rigid like a book, her cigarette its ribbon, but the open window didn't let in a breeze or let out the smoke. She stubbed it in her large orange ashtray and took my brother away for his wash.

"Mita, can I get a bottle of water? With some Lemos in?" With the bottle in my sweaty hand I left the house by the back door, closed the screen softly and stepped onto the hot concrete block paving, up onto the planters, where all the plants had died after Christmas, and onto the wall. It was painted green on our side and yellow on theirs but otherwise the houses were identical.

I tapped on the window of Rebecca's room. She was in her pyjamas already but she smiled and nodded. She caught up to me a few minutes later where the street runs out of houses. We were headed to our tree. It was the farthest you could go inside the fence this way and was just out of sight of the houses. We climbed up to our platform, made from half a door we had salvaged from the barracks a few years previously; it was a careful climb past thorns and sharp bark. She brought out birthday cake wrapped in foil. I hugged her.

"Happy birthday Rebecca."

"Are you feeling better?"

"Still a bit hot. Did you win?"

"Of course." We toasted her again, the 1985 200m sprint champion. She drank from the bottle and I had the cap. "To my last race as an under-thirteen."

"Was he there?" She knew I meant *him*. They always sent a conscript on board, and somehow it was often just him.

"Well, I sat next to him in the plane. But him and the pilot stayed outside somewhere while we were having the races." She sounded quite out of breath and I was still light headed. And then another sound, low rumbling. The setting sun was reddening the desert rocks when a truck lumbered past. Four people sat in the front and the brown vehicle waltzed from side to side like an old woman. Predicting where the army trucks went was an old game of ours.

"He said he may have to go out. Maybe he's with them."

"Why would he?"

"Well, he didn't have to do anything today really — just coming along with the school isn't hard work."

The road curved from the gate that we couldn't see, past us and then straight toward the hills, sharp etched stone coloured against the sky.

"It can't be for fighting, not if they're alone."

"And there's nothing on the back, no guns or anything."

"Is it a secret, do you think?"

"It's always a secret."

"Like, why are they fighting against the black people anyway?"

"Because they're communists."

"Not all. Mita's black and she's been living with us for such a long time, and she's not a communist."

"You can't tell just by looking, you know."

"Maybe they're just fetching something, if they aren't taking anything." The truck faded from brown to gun grey.

How long was it before we saw the lights of the army truck again? The full moon was up but the earth was still hot and Rebecca had said that she wanted to go home. I still burned. That makes it longer than an hour and less than two when the truck returned and kicked dust our way on the turn. The dry smell made me sneeze. We climbed down, took our turns hugging the tree and climbing down. The nubbin of tree resin that I knocked off tasted salty, as fresh blood does, as tears do, and I moved it around my mouth by tongue. Rebecca yawned as we parted. I waited and then I followed the fence. The soldiers had climbed out and stood there, all of them pale, silvery pale and carefully not touching one another though they had been sitting thigh to thigh moments before. But he wasn't one of them. The truck had stopped outside one of the long buildings, its back facing the double doors.

I waited in the shadow as they took their brown shirts off and washed their arms up to the soft bit just above the elbow taking turns holding the fire hose. "A clean shirt and a beer," one of them said and they all agreed. "And then we can come finish here." What was under the tarpaulin, what had they been to fetch?

I found a loose corner and lifted the heavy fabric with both hands. There was an awful smell but I couldn't make out what it was, not at first. Feet? Shouldn't be here on legs lying still in a row. I lifted further to let the moon shine in and saw the fullness of feet and legs, black legs, dead black legs attached to dead black men with pants pushed up and no boots, but feet that usually wore them. I was shivering and tears came and moaning and I shrank with the cold, stepped backwards into the shadow. I wouldn't turn my back to that death. From farther I could see the outlines; the truck was full of bodies, ten or fifteen shapes.

Then all smell disappeared, my knees were numb

and, though I knew every road in the camp, I got lost in my head as my view wavered, like trying to see out of a bathroom window and, suddenly, I was home. I wiped my eyes and walked in the front door.

"Marie, where have you been?" my dad asked. "I thought you were sleeping." I walked on. To bed. I thought I would be awake for some time, sucked the tree gum and shuddered under my spare blanket. Until I quieted down and slept.

nature of theft:

It was nighttime in Stellenbosch and I was speaking to someone outside away from the music. She had been invited to the party by the host, but she didn't know him well. It was a psychobabble stream of consciousness conversation in a tiny suburban garden sitting in rattan chairs with the glass sliding door behind us, between us and the party. She told me about being an outsider and where and when she thinks it started for her. The worst part of the story, the part that I remember in vivid detail, is this story that she told me.

covers

rusty harris

Mario's late again.

Last Saturday he didn't show at JR's until the second set. He got a big hand, though, leaping on stage like a twenty-year-old, his big smile still white, his hair as full as in high school, the fucker. I'd turned my back to the audience and whispered, "You make me sing lead again and I'll kick your dick in the dirt," but he just stepped up to the mike and said, "This next one's for the redhead in the blue over by the bar," and swung into "Crazy Little Thing Called Love."

So the clock over the bar shows 7:40, which means it's 7:30 and we go on at 8:00. We've been playing here at The Relic House off and on for going on thirty years, so it's not like he's lost. Every band's got one, that's all: a Mario. You start out playing in their garage, so they're in charge, even at 14. Lead singers, man.

I booked tonight's gig with the owner, Clam, about three months ago. His place, The Relic House, is a hole.

It's all decorated with road signs and all that other shit everybody's got now — hockey sticks and pictures of movie stars — except Clam did the whole found objects deal before anybody else. Maybe that's why everything's so damn dusty.

The place is a warren of rooms, one with a juke, another with a pool table and pinball, all leading to the biggest space in the back where there's a bar. Mismatched chairs pull up to 50s' Formica tables between the bar and the stage, just leaving enough room for dancing. The Relic House isn't the worst place we've played, but at this point, all the gigs pretty much look the same, down to the weary waitresses — either too old or too young — carrying drink-laden trays heavy as Sisyphus' rock.

From force of habit, I walk to the back where the pay phone still hangs on the wall between the two bathrooms — an unintended relic, I guess. I pull out my cell and punch in Mario's number. While it rings, Emil and Stevie push through the front door to start unloading and setting up. Stevie carries in his cymbal bags first, one in each hand to balance himself because they're so damn heavy. Maybe that's why drummers are so big. Stevie's got a big gut, but his arms are friggin' pistons and his leg muscles strain at the seams of his Levi's.

Stevie and I exchange a look when Emil plugs into his tube amp, an old piece of crap Emil says produces a great sound except when it doesn't. They add their cases to mine next to the stage where some drunk's always dancing too close and falling into them. Emil props his Fender on its stand and walks over to get a drink.

He leans over the counter and Bonnie, a tiny blonde, gives him a quick kiss and reaches around to tug at his graying ponytail. Bonnie's okay. She's got her sad tale like everybody, a houseful of kids, a bunch of exes and no child support, but she's real sweet. And she's a good bartender, always making sure to send over a tray of beers before every set. When Jen comes, which is less and less, she and Bonnie usually hang out.

Watching Bonnie and Emil, I realize I'm really waiting for Jen. I listen to a few more hollow rings, then snap the phone closed and climb the stage to talk to Stevie.

"Hey, man," Stevie says, hunched over, his cocked ear listening to his fingers tapping the skins. The sheen on his balding head matches the fittings on his drums. His hair is long on the sides, and it hangs, thin and anemic, in his face.

"Mario's late," I say.

Stevie pulls a drum key out of his pocket and starts tuning the snare. Grayish fuzz sprouts from his ears. We're all getting fucking old. I don't look in the mirror if I can help it, but my balls dangle more than they used to, my ass has almost disappeared, I've got these weird creases near my sideburns I gotta watch out for when I shave, and not one day goes by when I don't have an ache or pain somewhere.

"God, I hate singing lead."

Stevie looks up. "He might show. It's only a quarter of."

My gear is on stage, ready to go. I keep a good eye on my Gibson. I paid $200 in 1969 and it's probably worth four or five times that now.

A few customers trickle in. It's always the same. Old bikers, old ex-druggies and ex-hippies. People addicted to their hogs or assholes that follow the Grateful Dead from town to town or women trussing their stretch marks and sag into teenage clothes, still wearing their hair long and straight, parted in the middle. They drink a lot, they tip well, and we know what they want to hear. I used to try originals with them, excited to try out the new stuff. The dance floor'd clear, the conversation drowned us out, and people would start calling out for songs they wanted to hear. I dial Mario's number again.

By 8:15, Clam's already been over twice asking why we aren't getting started, so we trudge on up and get to it. My normal voice is raspy and I try to imagine I can get a sexy Tom Waits type of thing going, but at best I sound like Randy Newman with a lousy case of the flu. Stevie and Emil are good guys and give me back up, but I am seriously pissed at Mario.

By the third set, I'm tired. I used to be able to stand for hours, but my legs are sore. Some days it doesn't feel any different to stand on a stage or stand on an assembly line. I keep wishing Jen would show.

"You know what, Mitch?" she'd said last week. "I think the water heater's done for."

I'm below the waist, trailing my fingers along her C-section scar and she's examining the ends of her hair, smoking a cigarette.

"I'll look at it this weekend."

The view from where I am kind of doubles her chin.

"Are you coming on Saturday?" I ask, resting my

cheek on her thigh.

"Oh, I don't know."

"You used to really like going. You're still my groupie, right?"

"Yeah, hon."

It's after 10:00. At the next break, I walk to the back to call Mario again. A skinny brunette in tight pink jeans with her blouse tied up under her breasts is already leaning against the wall talking into her cell. She smiles at me with her eyebrows raised. My eyes drop to her tired, slack belly.

"Don't use the stove, you hear?" she says into the phone. "Just the microwave."

She hangs up and starts to squeeze past me. "You're in the band," she says, putting a hand on my upper arm, maybe to flirt, probably to steady herself.

"Yeah," I say. "Excuse me," I add, but she's wandered off.

Mario's still not home. I bang the phone closed, and then open it and punch in my own number. I'll just ask her to come for the last set and then we'll go to that expensive deli on Ventura, the one with all the famous people stuffing themselves with pastrami at 2 a.m. It seems weird that the endless repeated ringing sounds exactly the same whether I'm calling Mario or Jen.

Emil's amp completely screws up in the fourth set. We're doing "You Are So Beautiful" and the floor's full of slow dancers when the amp starts freaking out. It emits ear-wrenching static until Emil whomps it a couple of times.

"Jesus," I snarl.

Emil turns red. "Sorry," he mutters.

The cement sensation in my legs builds. The glare on the stage blasts us into a sweaty blindness. I can see the bar across the room, but the dance floor is a blur of jeans and cigarette smoke and jerky movement — a tired dry hump in the dark. We do "Go Your Own Way" and thump wearily into "Sunshine of Your Love."

"Hey!" slurs a little dude by my feet. He's got his hands on the stage, grasping at my boots with big-knuckled hands, gray with dirt, covered with scrapes and nicks. Stevie bangs his sticks together to count off the next song, but this guy, this freaky short guy, keeps yelling "Hey!" until I think I'm gonna kick *his* dick in the dirt.

I raise my arm and Stevie holds up.

I squint down at the guy. "What?"

"Play slomotonwachter!" he wails. I can see way too much of the inside of his mouth, which is a loose open pouch, wet and blurred. He smells of cheap scotch and decaying teeth and something both meaty and sour.

I can't understand what he's slurring, but he keeps repeating until I can make a stab at it.

"Man, we don't know that one," I try, holding my head at an awkward angle to avoid his breath.

"Slomotonwachter! Slomotonwachter!"

I look at Stevie and Emil. "We've got a request. Anybody know 'Slomotonwachter'?"

Stevie shakes his head and smiles. Emil's feelings are still hurt about the amp, so he just stares at the wall behind the bar. He's always been this way, ever since high school; sensitive, I guess, but I'll apologize later.

"Sorry, man," I say to the tiny drunk, shifting my feet away from his clutching hands. "We don't know that one. You'll like the one we're gonna do, though."

The jerk refuses to be placated. He puts his hands on his hips stubbornly and yells, but more slowly. "Slowmotionwalter! Slowmotionwalter!"

I look for Clam to come throw the guy out, but he's nowhere. I nod to Stevie and he counts down for "Old Time Rock & Roll" and we play it but this guy keeps it up through the whole song. A couple of people boo, and someone calls, "Shut the fucker up!"

Over the light applause at the end of the number, the guy's still at it. "Slow Motion Walter! Slow Motion Walter!"

A muscular dude wearing a Levi's jacket with torn-out arms grabs the guy from behind and lifts him from the floor. The little guy goes ballistic, flailing his arms and kicking backward into the other guy's shins. Where the fuck is Clam?

"It's okay, it's okay," I say. "Put him down, okay? Thanks. Thanks. Shit. Okay. How does it go, man?" I ask, crouching at the edge of the stage. My knees snap and crackle like friggin' cereal.

The little guy's buggy eyes roll around in his slack, mottled face. The smell is so bad. The biker shakes his head and goes back to his beer.

"C'mon, just tell me so we can play it," I tell the stinky guy.

"Slow Motion Walter!" he whines, like a kid throwing a supermarket tantrum.

"Yeah, but how does it go? Can you sing some?" Emil steps closer for this, and Stevie lifts up from his stool.

The freak lifts his torn-up hands toward the ceiling and his mouth works. At first nothing comes up, and then with a great effort, he croaks, "DAH DAH

DAH… DAH DAH dah DAH… ”

Emil hoots. Stevie falls back on his throne so hard he almost tips over. Then he cracks up. “He’s not saying Slow Motion Walter — ” he chokes.

I pat the freak’s arm. “Got it, man.”

I nod at the guys. Stevie chants, “One… two… one, two, three, four,” and Emil whangs down on his Fender, and we blast into a song we haven’t played since Mario’s garage.

We play it, we play “Smoke on the Water,” and I howl it out. I remember most of the words, surprising myself. On the first chorus, I move to Emil’s mike and we sing it together. We’re cracking up, all of us, especially when the whole room joins in. By the end of the song, they’re screaming it, the AM radio schlocky piece of crap. The freaky little dude holds onto the edge of the stage, swaying, a big slobbery smile on his face, until he finally passes out on the instrument cases. I play the big organ ending on my Gibson because we don’t have keyboards. All those songs and their hooks, they’re engrained. When we hit the last note, the place erupts. Everyone wants to buy the band a beer, but we just sip at a few while we accept high fives and back slaps. Stevie’s got a little liver trouble, and I don’t need to add more gut, and we’ve all got the drive home.

We pack it up at 2:30: Emil’s bass and shitty tube amp, my Gibson, Stevie’s kit. The three of us stop at Denny’s on the way home. I tell Emil I’m sorry, and Stevie makes us listen to the only joke he can remember, the one about cannibals eating a clown.

I order the pastrami to honor Jen’s no-show and it tastes like crap.

Stevie's cell rings just as we're leaving. "Yeah," he says. He listens and then says, "OK, right."

He shoves the phone in his pocket and plucks a toothpick from the holder next to the cash register. "That was Mario. He'll see us at the Green Room gig tomorrow night."

We push through the doors and stand on the sidewalk. The parking lot's just about empty. The mown grass surrounding the restaurant looks impossibly smooth and perfect. In the flowerbeds, red and orange masses of impatiens spill over their boundaries, threatening to overtake the lawn. I can never get mine to grow like that.

nature of theft:

I love my ex-husband's sister. Although ten years younger, Belinda's the one I want to be with — a tasty mélange of old soul, stand-up comic, and wide-eyed teen. Her stories rock, but I didn't steal one of hers.

Like the genius she is, she waited until the perfect person came along and then snagged him. Mitch is funny, warm, edgy… and musical. He fit like a T-shirt bra, or a pair of snuggly socks, or some other cottony undergarment. Our threesome became a foursome.

Mitch played bass with rock bands for years, and like my husband, another musician, Mitch has some great stories.

One night, Mitch, Belinda, my husband and I were shooting the shit, admiring my springtime garden (and tactfully ignoring the telephone wires and power lines crisscrossing the backyard) when Mitch told the story of Slow Motion Walter, one of his many adventures while playing with one of a zillion cover bands. I tell it here, fictionalized, but the core is pure Mitch.

Mitch and Belinda ditched us for the pine woods of Oregon, so maybe my theft of one of his best stories can be forgiven? I miss him, man.

one story only

alison miller

The grass is wet enough at this time of the morning to get the marmalade off. Most of it. Only the dog shit to watch for. Then I sit on the rim of the waterless fountain, well out of sight of the clinic, and take the rest of the stickiness off with baby wipes. Right foot first. I rest it yogi-style, sole up on my left thigh. I use one wipe for the sole and another for between the toes where the marmalade has squelched up. Two for the inside of my shoe, making sure no bits of peel are left stuck along the edge between the upper and the sole. Then I slip my foot in. Same process with the left. It feels good when I stand up in my shoes again, feet clean and tingling in the cold.

I take each piece of toast by what's left of the crust, go round the fountain, keep the hedge and the trees between me and the clinic, and cross to the concrete basin. After school it's full of kids on bikes and skateboards, but it's deserted now. Every night the old Sikh with the white turban walks round the edge and scatters a yellow circle of nan bread, chapati and saffron rice for the pigeons. I tear each slice of toast into four and drop the pieces at regular intervals round the circle, so no one will notice them. The nurses haven't caught on so far. They check my bag, but never think of looking in my shoes. They think the economy pack of baby wipes is just part of my problem. Another wipe for my hands then, and I collect all the used ones and drop them into one of the new metal bins.

I take another look round. You can't be too careful. I wouldn't put it past my mother to have her spies out; she knows a few people this side of Glasgow. But it's early yet and I have the park more or less to myself. The only folk about are the four or five stressed-out office workers doing Tai Chi in the lea of the hedge that runs alongside the herbaceous border. They move in slow motion, straining to hold back the day.

Now I can relax for a bit before I go back. I sit on a bench in front of the border and stare at the black earth turned and ready for planting. I prefer it like this. In the summer when the poppies riot along with the lilies and geraniums and peonies and lupins it's too much for me. Too loud. A cacophony of colour.

More and more these days, my mind goes back to Poland. You can move halfway around the world. You can move all the way round the world. Still it follows you. I only got as far as Glasgow, but at the time I thought it was far enough.

In my memory the first part of that day detaches itself from the rest, its atmosphere so different. At first

I was uneasy as my mother thumped about the kitchen muttering: Hand mills VERBOTEN; *baking bread* VERBOTEN; *feeding your family* VERBOTEN! *I didn't know what verboten meant, but I knew it wasn't Polish. I knew it had something to do with the German soldiers in the village. Anger blazing in her eyes, she retrieved the pieces of the hand mill from their hiding places. Her movements were quick and determined. One stone, the one with the hole in the middle for the grain and the smaller hole at the side for the handle, she pulled from the far side of the barn, under the hay. The wooden handle was tied to the top of a beam with a piece of sacking. Up the wooden steps to the attic she thumped, and hauled the other stone from the corner next to the chimney. She came down backwards, the stone clutched to her breast with one hand.*

That day I could not keep my eyes off my mother. She heaved the stones inside, set them on the floor, then stood up with a big smile on her face. The more she worked, the more cheerful she became. Finally she assembled the mill and dragged the sack of grain into the house. As she ground it into flour, turning the handle, letting grain trickle from her cupped hand, a cloud rose around us, gold in the light of the stove in the warm kitchen, separating us from the rest of the world; from the freezing cold and the snow that obliterated the countryside and piled up against the houses.

Once she had mixed the flour into dough and set it to rise by the stove, she started singing to herself like she used to before the war, quiet and dreamy. Her face glowed in the light of the flames when she bent to stoke the fire. The lines disappeared and she looked as beautiful and holy as the saints in the village church. She hardly noticed I was there.

I sit hunched on the bench till the workers and school kids have filed past and the dog walkers have taken possession of the park, standing about in twos and threes comparing notes about their precious pooches. The Chinese women with their square cut grey hair, are doing their exercises, stretching and swinging their arms, sturdy legs in baggy trousers, feet firmly planted. They communicate in Cantonese, a loud singsong. It must be good to be able to talk and know that only the people you want to can understand you. Up at the clinic, the walls have ears. There's a saying among the girls: *Careless talk costs pounds.* If the staff get a whiff of your strategies to avoid food, you'll have big Nurse Baxter on your case for days, sitting on your bed spooning porridge into you till you're 'back on course'.

Time to go. They'll have searched my room by now for the toast they're not convinced I've really eaten, despite the decoy bits of crust I've left on my plate. And I still have my 'homework' to do for the psychologist. I prise my frozen legs from the bench and set off stiffly up the hill, the long way round to avoid the weeping ash. On the bank daffodils nod perversely in the icy wind that pares me to the bone.

The loaf was in the oven ten minutes when they crashed through the door and caught my mother dismantling the mill. Her face went white again. My father came running in after them waving his arms helplessly. When they dragged her out through the door into the snow, all I remember thinking was, I hope the bread won't burn before we get back.

Just up from the house is a row of skinny birches. In the slanting sun they stand, shivering white limbs on the edge of a ravine. Two of the soldiers look at them; pretend to size them up; say something to my father, who stands holding the ladder, shaking his head. My mother is on her knees trembling in the snow; the rope around her middle pins her arms to her sides; her black skirt is powdered white. The biggest soldier jerks her to her feet.

Further up is an ancient ash, the height and girth of a cathedral pillar, holding up the sky at the edge of the forest. It has a horizontal branch ten feet up. The oldest soldier undoes the rope from round my mother and slings it over the branch. Snow showers down on us. He speaks again to my father who hands him the ladder. He sets it against the tree under the branch.

As soon as I step in through the wide door of the clinic, I forget my homework. A couple of the girls are talking in low voices in the common room to the right of the hall. I take my shoes off so they won't hear them clacking on the marble tiles and pull me in to swap stories of meals avoided, regurgitated or dispatched down the Swanney with laxatives. Without planning to, I sneak down the corridor to the left of the oak staircase towards Sister Rita's room. This part of the clinic is a throwback to the time when it was run by nuns and there is a plaster Virgin Mary in a niche, inclining her head to look at me as I pass.

Sister Rita says, "Come in," as soon as I knock, in

that bright silver voice of hers, eager for company. A leftover, she calls herself. The clinic still has links with the Sisters of Perpetual Sorrow, or whatever the order is, and they allowed her to stay on when the day-to-day running was taken over by health professionals. She's well into her nineties now, tiny and birdlike. It's her eyes I always notice first: they're enormous and bathe you in blue light. Or that's how it seems. She sits in her old green armchair swathed in crocheted blankets, her head nodding continuously as if she approves thoroughly of everything she sees. Our Lady of Perpetual Affirmation, I call her to amuse the other girls.

But privately I wish she was my grandmother, and sometimes I pretend she is.

"Well, Ewa, have the birds had a good breakfast?" she asks as soon as I sit down. "Are there lots of plump sparrows and blue tits and overfed blackbirds in the park today?" Straight to the point. Nothing much escapes those luminous eyes. At first it alarmed me, till I realised she wasn't going to tell the staff.

Now I think, just please don't mention crows.

The third soldier looked about sixteen. Jan's age. Jan had been with the partisans for a year. He'd stopped coming back to persuade Father to join them. Last time he came, he spat his contempt at my father's lame excuses. Mother did not intervene in the argument, but after Jan had gone, she set down the cured pork she had been saving in front of Father, who kept his eyes on his plate and said nothing.

What would Jan say when he found out about Mother?

Even at nine years old I could tell the third soldier wasn't in on the joke. He was white as pork fat under his helmet; a big red spot stuck out on his neck; his collar was too big and stood stiffly back from the spot. There was more starch in his uniform than in him. He looked as if he might collapse in a boneless heap any minute. Why didn't my father grab his rifle and shoot the other two before it was too late?

But he doesn't. He stands there, my father, with me and the young German, the three of us rooted in the snow. The other two soldiers smoke and laugh, watching my mother's frantic dance at the end of the rope. One of them flaps his arms and jumps from foot to foot in imitation.

"Alte, schwarze Krähe!" *he says.*

I didn't understand the German then and had to ask my father.

"Old — black — crow," she would say, enunciating each word slowly, as she dished out my tea, or eyed my uneaten bread. "Your grandmother was thirty-three when they hanged her. The age I was when you were born."

Even after she had stopped jerking, I looked up at Mother a long time to see if she would move again. The oldest soldier gave an order to the boy and Father and I watched him run down to the house. A few minutes later he came back cradling the hot round loaf. It looked ready. Still, my mother would have tapped it with her middle finger to make sure it was baked right through.

The older soldiers laughed at the terror on the boy's face when one of them stuck his bayonet in the loaf, swung it out of his grasp in a wide arc and hurled it into the snow beneath my mother's dangling feet. Then the two of them turned their backs and pissed on it. I couldn't take my eyes off Mother's loaf, steaming and stinking in the snow.

When they'd buttoned themselves up again, they turned and said: "Jetzt essen Sie, bitte." *And they bowed deeply.*

"Ewa, are you *list*-ening to me?" She would always sound the 't', an echo of a mother tongue clotted with consonants. As if she was trying to en*list* me into her view of the world. "Now eat, please."

" ...And you know, even Nurse Baxter is not so bad." Sister Rita's silvery voice drifts back into focus and her blue eyes fix me. "She means well." Her head is nodding in emphasis.

Yes, I know. But every time she looks at me it's fear I see. And disgust. When she pushes, tray first, into my room, they're written all over her face.

They said they would shoot anyone who tried to remove the body that night. Next day at dawn my father cut her down and carried her back to the house. My mother was frozen solid; her dress was stiff as a board.

He laid her on the wooden table, where we ate every day, where she had kneaded the dough. As she thawed out, her black clothes dripped and steamed in the warmth and released the final treacherous stink her body had made. Her face remained blue.

When the old wife came to wash her down, I was sent to the other end of the house. I could still hear my father's sobs and the old wife crooning some ancient Polish song.

As if she needed a lullaby, my mother, who would sleep forever now.

"Ewa, Ewa, Ewa," my father said over and over, crying softly.

I don't want to leave Sister Rita's room. It feels safe in here. But Dr Baird has threatened to 'review' my 'contract', because I've put on no weight at all and my periods haven't come back.

"What age are you, Ewa?" he asks.

"I'll be thirty this year."

"Is it not time you started to invest in life?" he says, exasperated. "Before it's too late?"

So, I'd better show willing and take part in some of the groups. At least it's not Reminiscence Therapy today. They have some notion they can 'reconnect you to positive aspects of your childhood'.

"What stories do you remember being told?"

They go round the circle and the girls call out: The Gingerbread Man; Goldilocks and The Three Bears; The Little Red Hen...

Then they come to me. "What about you, Ewa?"

I shake my head.

nature of theft:

There are at least four thefts I can identify in One Story Only, but the one that forms the core narrative came from a man called Jan Krawczyk. In 1992 or 93 he came to my office in Castlemilk to ask for help to publish his war memoir, a vivid account of various daring escapes from the Germans he had made as a boy in Poland. At the time I worked for the Workers Educational Association running adult education classes in creative writing and local history. Though I tried and gave various suggestions, I couldn't help him achieve his goal of publication and I haven't seen or heard from him since.

One throwaway sentence in the manuscript stayed with me. It went something like, "The use of handmills was forbidden and women caught working them were hanged." It struck me as incredibly powerful that something as archetypally life-giving as milling flour to bake bread should lead to death. Years later I wrote the story. I told myself that if it was ever published, I would try to contact Jan Krawczyk and own up. But I have no idea where he lives, or even if he is still alive.

I also stole his name. One of my characters is called Jan. Another is Ewa, pronounced Evva. I stole it from Ewa Wojciechowska, the Group Analyst on a course I was doing at the time I wrote the story. I trawled the net for other Polish names but these seemed to fit best.

The fourth theft is the title, One Story Only, which comes from a line in a Margaret Atwood poem sequence, Four Small Elegies, describing how in 1838, after a failed uprising in what is now Quebec, the British army burned the houses and barns of the civilian population around Beauharnois, driving them out into the snow to freeze to death. The third of these elegies contains the idea that certain experiences are so horrific that the life of the survivor becomes the telling and retelling of that trauma.

Admitting to these thefts I don't even touch on what some think of as the central moral dilemma of the fiction writer: when writing about lives they haven't lived, are authors driven by imagination and empathy to capture and illuminate the experience of being human; or is it appropriation, pure and simple?

i would never eat a tapir

sarah salway

For Caroline

"Of course, we might never get it right."

She's not sure she's heard him properly, but now the taxi driver is asking "North or South?" and she's double checking the tickets, passports and he's putting on his glasses because he says it's the only way he can get through security without being stopped. He says they make him look vulnerable, but when she looks at him, he seems more like a man she might once have found attractive. Like finding a photograph of a teenage boyfriend and being nostalgic for the heartbroken diary entries he caused rather than the relationship itself. Perhaps this is why she forgets to ask him what he meant.

An elderly man is standing in the middle of International Departures. It's hard to fathom his expression as every item in his bag is taken out and examined. Three radios, in scruffy, well-handled boxes, are already lined up on the side, and then the books are fished out, their pages rifled through and held up as if the pony-tailed airport official expects something to fall out. Lastly, handfuls of biros appear. One escapes the clutches of the official and clatters down to Rebecca's feet. She bends down to pick it up, and after hesitating, tries to hand it back to the man.

He looks surprised, before nodding towards the official. Rebecca leaves the pen on the side. She doesn't want any part in this. It feels unclean in a way it wouldn't if the man complained or sighed; showed, in any way, that this wasn't how he expected to be treated.

Rebecca picks up her bag from the security belt and looks round for Malcolm. She sees him arguing with an official by the corner screens. He's taken off his glasses and one of his hands is slicing the air but the other is holding something she can't make out. He looks like he's waving layers of pink tissue in the air. She edges closer, but then she realises what it is.

"Malcolm," she shouts.

When he turns round, she sees he's not annoyed but is smiling, and as he stuffs the tutu back into the bag, the official winks at her, cuffing Malcolm on the arm. Man to man.

"Were you talking about me?" she asks, when they walk into the departure lounge to be hit by the shops, the restaurants, the signs. For a moment, she wonders if this is where they're supposed to be arriving at, rather than just another stop on the way.

"I might have been. Shall we get some breakfast?"

She sighs, not sure how she's going to survive the next

four days.

The plane has only been in the air five minutes before she starts to cry.

"The tutu story is mine," she says. "I told you it, but it's still my story. You will not make it yours. You will not."

Malcolm just shakes his head, so Rebecca looks out of the plane window. She thinks of the man at the airport, and his face as he watched his bag being unpacked. The books weren't even classics, or new. And she could have sworn the biro she picked up had been chewed.

"It was supposed to be a surprise. To make you laugh," he whispers, pushing his glasses back on his nose after they both manage to get through customs without being stopped.

She huffs. Even she can see it's the only word for it. And that does make her laugh, so by the time the Swedish taxi driver points out the building where only two nights before they'd presented the Nobel Prizes, both of them want to stop. They walk up and down outside holding hands, wondering what it might be like to be so great, so special. Clear, she thinks, unmuddled. Like the ice that's covering the black water in front of them.

"You can go in," says the taxi driver, pointing at the door. "In Sweden everything is open."

But neither of them want it to be that easy.

Stockholm is auditioning for a role in a child's snowglobe. The steep lanes in the old town are glistening with snow, and they have to hold on to each other as they slide their way from the hotel down to the harbour.

"Lunch soon. What do you want to eat?" he asks.

She can't stop wondering why they both just threw their bags on the bed in the hotel room before coming out. Shouldn't they have jumped on each other? They're young, free and in Stockholm after all. "In Sweden," she mimics, "everything is open." Apart from us, she adds to herself. That bloody tutu. It's become an elephant in the room. What does he expect her to do with it? Model it for him, maybe, so he can watch her become the little dancer she'd always wanted to be. Does he really think he can give her a happy childhood twenty-five years too late? What little she glimpsed of it was pretty though. Not a real dancing one obviously. This was soft, not stiff. A flutter of glittering pink snowflakes

"I'd like to see where ABBA live," she says brightly, "or go on a boat."

"We could have reindeer balls," he says. "Now that's something I've always wanted to try."

Even though it's lunchtime, there are candles on every table in the restaurant.

"Real meat," he's saying. "That's what we all need. Humans aren't designed to have our meals just put in front of us but to go out and find it. We should have to work for our food. It's the hunter complex."

The waiter puts their plates in front of them. Two large spherical balls sit in a puddle of red juice.

"They're not really, are they?" she says, but stops when she sees him laughing.

"Oh, please tell me you didn't think… " he splutters.

She spears one of the meatballs with her fork — a spray of oil spurts over her plate and into her glass. She watches the oil drip down, then curdle, leaving a greasy film over the top of the water. Three days, fourteen hours left.

After lunch, and back in the bedroom, they lie side by side, not touching, staring up at the ceiling. Ever since he told her about the quiet time his mother used to make him have in the afternoon, it's the time she likes best. To lie with him, the room darkened and the clock stilled so when they get up, they're shocked to realise the world has been going on without them.

"Sushi," she says, after they've been silent too long. "You love sushi and you don't exactly fight for that, do you? Well, unless you call taking a plate off a conveyor belt hard work."

She's thinking of the conveyor belt at the airport, and the man who just stood there. She won't tell Malcolm the story though. He'd enjoy it too much. By the time, he'd finished dissecting the reasons for the man's luggage, it will be Malcolm's school in Africa that's being furnished, Malcolm's large family of home-schooled children who have never seen a biro, Malcolm's underground bartering system in which a radio is the equivalent of four cows. By the time Malcolm had devoured him, the man would have nothing left.

He rolls over until he's on top of her. "It's you who is hard work," he says, wiping the hair from her face, and kissing her first on one cheek and then the other, before he finds her mouth. He rests his lips only millimetres from hers so she can feel the vibration of his words. "I should just grab you by the hair and pull you wherever I want you to go."

"And I suppose actually adding up all the sushi plates at the end is part of this same big hunting instinct."

He takes a lock of her hair and rubs it across his upper lip so it makes him look as if he's got a moustache. It's something that makes her laugh usually. "Grr," he says, but even he would admit it's more of a mewl than a growl.

"Oh fuck," she says, pushing him off.

"That had been the general idea," he says, picking up the hotel's tourist guide to Stockholm.

Three days, nine hours and still they haven't mentioned the tutu.

On a trip out to the islands, the boat stops at one of the remotest to let an elderly couple off.

"They're artists," the female guide explains. "They will stay in one of the summer houses for a couple of days to paint. Mad people." She mock shudders with the cold, but Rebecca rushes to the other side of the boat so she can wave to the couple. They're both shouldering equally large bags, and don't look back.

Back in the harbour, he puts both arms round her and swings her ashore. "Right," he says, "let's look at you." He undoes her scarf and winds it round her neck again, pulls her hat down so her ears are covered, makes her hold out her hands so he can check her gloves, and lastly buttons and unbuttons her coat. Then he holds out one arm so she can shelter under it, and kisses the top of her head.

She'd normally be angry at being treated like a child, but today, in the snow, she doesn't care. She nestles next to him, pressing one hand into his pocket. "So, shall we go and find ABBA?" he asks.

It isn't long before they give up the hunt, and go in search of hot chocolate instead.

"Is there any animal you wouldn't eat?" she asks, licking her spoon and holding the hot metal against her nose.

He wipes a fleck of chocolate off her chin before he answers. "I would never eat a tapir," he says. "That would be just plain cruel and unnecessary."

"Why are we here?" she asks, putting the spoon down with a clang.

"You remind me of a tapir," he says. "Ungainly and scared. And then there's the nose of course. So I'd probably never eat you. You're safe."

"Ungainly?" She presses her palm up to her nose and squashes it flat.

"We wanted to get away," he says. "We both agreed Stockholm was different."

"Probably?"

He makes a face at her. "It is different, isn't it?" he asks. "I mean everyone else has Paris. But not us, we will have herring, ice and animal testicles for ever more."

"You just said you'd only *probably* never eat me."

"Don't take everything so literally," he says. "Shall I tell you a secret?"

She nods.

"I used to love singing along to ABBA with Mum. We even had a dance routine we'd do together. It was probably one of the worst days of my life when I realised that it wasn't cool to know all the words."

"And that was really the worst day of your life? I give up." She shrugs.

He's holding the mug so tight she can see his knuckles have gone white, and there's a sudden chill in the air. "Of course not," he says. "That would be the day my mother was caught entertaining."

She doesn't breathe, just stares at him. He's talked about his mother before, but never what he really felt about her. After years of trying to get him to open up, now she's frightened of what might happen.

"It was my fault," he says, looking up at her finally. "I should have stopped him, the lover boy, but instead I just waved him on in to the house knowing my father was there too. Roll up, roll up, one and all into the lion's den. I was too busy concentrating on how jealous my brother was going to be because I was first to sit in the new car Dad had just driven home."

"Do it,' she says. 'Ask me to marry you."

He hasn't taken his eyes off her. She puts her hand over his where it's still clutching the mug.

"Now," she says.

He shakes his head, once for a negative, and then again and again as if he's trying to get rid of the thoughts. The relief of not being fixed by his gaze is replaced by a hunger she doesn't understand. She wants to hit him, but clenches her free hand again and again under the table instead.

"Malcolm, your mother would have gone anyway," she says, as calmly as she can. "You were only, what, four when she left home. You couldn't have stopped her."

"I know." He slips his fingers from hers and starts

putting on his gloves. "After all, over the years I've paid therapists thousands of pounds just to be able to say those words without feeling guilty. Now, shall we go? There's a national treasure of a castle to visit if I'm not mistaken."

They run back to the hotel to escape the cold. The tips of each wool glove finger have frozen where she has been sucking them, and her cheeks are stinging.

In the bedroom, she stands in front of the mirror staring at her reflection.

"What are you thinking?" he calls from the bathroom, where he's shaving. She waves briefly so she can see her reflection greeting his, and the reflection of their reflection and so on. Hundreds of hers waving at hundreds of him. None of them saying anything.

"You called me ungainly," she says at last. It's this more than anything that has got her. He can't have forgotten about the ballet lessons she told him she'd begged and begged for, only to have to beg just as much to give them up after the teacher and the other pupils had laughed at her. "Two left feet apparently," her mother had repeated to her father at supper. "I'm so ashamed."

Rebecca had realised she'd never now be able to ask for the tutu the ballet lessons had been designed to get, and in that moment, she'd put all that sort of thing behind her, along with any hopes of ever being pretty, or wearing her hair in a perfect top knot, or being the sort of woman men worry about getting cold.

She stared hard at herself. A strong and capable woman. All in all, she'd been the winner, but it's good to be able to step over to the other side sometimes. Isn't that what the tutu in his bag is all about?

She moves to stand in the bathroom doorway.

"I bet you didn't really let them walk all over you," she says. "I bet you got your own back on your mother and your father and on everyone. Because if you hadn't done something, then all the therapy in the world wouldn't stop you feeling guilty."

She sees his eyes widen in the mirror, the rasp of the razor against his skin halting momentarily.

"You don't have to tell me but I bet it felt good, that terrible thing you did, didn't it?"

He nods then. A gesture so small she could have missed it if she didn't know where to look.

"Then it was the right thing to do," she says.

Afterwards, sated, they lie cradled in the huge ship-shaped bed, and she tells him about the man in the airport.

"I wonder what he was doing," she says, pausing to leave him room to take the story over, but he says nothing. He's tracing her collarbone from one side to the other, back and forth, stopping each time to rub the pad of his thumb up her neck. She can feel him press on her windpipe, but when she looks down at him, he's got his eyes shut.

"We should get up," she says, but she doesn't really care if they never leave the bed.

He springs up suddenly though, and she watches him as he runs naked across the room to his bag.

"Put it on." He hands her the tutu.

"Malcolm, I'm exhausted. Maybe later."

"No, put it on to wear out tonight. That's why I got it for you. When I saw it in the shop, I thought it would make you look like you could do anything."

"I'd look stupid."

"I'll be so proud of you. Besides, who cares? We're in Stockholm. Where everything is open."

As she holds the tutu against her, the layers crackle in her hands. When she looks through the net at him, it's as if he's in a pink snowglobe too. She says she can't again, but she knows she can, she will, and how much she wants to.

Even though she's wearing her coat, the petticoats of the tutu stick out. She holds them up with her arms straight as she walks down the stairs. If her mother were there, she'd do a pirouette right now. A perfect dainty turn.

Malcolm is waiting for her at the bottom. She almost expects him to clap, but he's staring up at the ceiling.

"Look," he says. "Look at the sky."

For a moment, she can't think what the polished timber planks are, but then she realises. There is a boat suspended by metal ropes from the hotel's atrium, so it's forever floating in the air. Underneath, looking up, they are at the bottom of the sea.

They try to find their way back to the building where the Nobel Prizes were presented, but the snow's coming down so thick now that they can't always work out the street signs on the map.

"Let's just give up," he says. "Go and find somewhere to eat."

"No." She's never been so determined. "Just five more minutes."

He traipses after her. "I'll tell you what I did do," he calls out, so she has to stop to listen. "The terrible thing

I did to my parents that day."

But she doesn't want to hear any more. She walks faster.

"Here it is." She raises one gloved hand up in a victory salute. "You see, you're right. This is a magical tutu. When I'm wearing it I have special powers. Just one of which being I can find my way to anywhere in the world."

She looks so pleased with herself, he doesn't mention that they've passed this building at least twice before that night but she hadn't listened to him when he tried to point it out.

They stand before the door the taxi driver told them was always open. She looks at the building, and up at the sky. There are no clouds, but the stars are so thickly layered she imagines they can take her weight too. Then she walks a couple of hundred metres away before turning to face him again. This time, she walks deliberately, but she still looks as if she's trying out someone else's footsteps for size. She sees finally what she was doing wrong all those years ago. When she starts to run, he holds out his arms and catches her. Her tutu billows up as he twirls her round.

"Of course," she says, as he puts her carefully back on solid ground, "we might never get it right."

"Who does?" he replies, pulling her hat down so her ears are fully covered.

nature of theft:

I Would Never Eat a Tapir was written for an acquaintance on her birthday as a surprise. Her best friend told me that my story should include the following five things — Tapir, Stockholm, Tutu, Sushi, and someone looking up at the sky. I didn't know this woman very well, but I had heard that my short story, The Quiet Hour, was one of her favourite short stories, so I made the main character, Malcolm, a grown up version of the small boy in my original story. It was the first time I'd 'stolen' one of my own characters and made them live again. I managed to weave in all the words but Tapir. I thought about cheating and using it as the title alone, but when I researched them on the internet their ungainliness struck a chord and changed Rebecca's personality in the story.

What those words meant to the recipient I have no idea, and it gave me an uncomfortable feeling when writing it — almost like reading her diary.

suck, blow

lauren simpson

Twenty-two hours. It took me twenty-two hours to put the new vacuum together, and it still didn't work right.

I didn't even labor on the baby that long, and halfway through those fifteen hours and thirty-seven minutes, I wanted God to strike me dead.

Sven, at least, had the decency to do what babies were supposed to do — sleep, cry, suck, crap, over and over again — after I'd worked so long putting her together. She slept, thumb rooted in her mouth, on a plastic-covered lawn cushion tucked out of the way in a corner of the den, while I grunted and sweat over the Bissell, flinging packaging all around the place and trying to fit Part A into Slot 1 — hell, trying to figure out which ones were the Part A and Slot 1 — the instructions were blabbing on about in Mexican. But Bobby had bought it for me that morning, and I knew he wasn't about to put it together. Bobby didn't give a damn how much dust was hiding in the shag.

I hadn't told him I wanted a new vacuum, hadn't so much as hinted — and you've got to do more than hint to make Bobby do anything, you've got to shout it from the windows with a bullhorn like what the announcer uses at the racetrack — but he brought it home just after ten, when the first of my soaps was starting, and said it was for me. A present. Something to keep my mind off the baby.

Truth be told, Sven wasn't bothering me. Tears, piss, vomit — nothing new when you're the oldest girl. Hers came in a smaller package, a fussy bundle of whimpers, but she was nothing I couldn't handle. I asked Bobby where he'd gotten the money, and he said it was a present, damn it, just put the fucking thing together and get off his back. Then he stomped out, started up the truck, and drove off to God-knew where.

So I did. Or I tried. I fit parts together in combinations that looked nothing like the pretty picture on the box, the photo that showed what a Bissell vacuum was supposed to look like, *could* look like when someone with half a grain of mechanical sense took a whack at the assembly, but nothing fit quite right. Sven woke at noon and started crying again, so I held her to one side, letting her suck while I studied the instruction manual and wondered why the vacuum couldn't be more like the baby.

Bobby didn't come home that night — a blessing, since I didn't want him to see vacuum parts scattered all over the room, blocking his path to the TV. I didn't want him watching the videos in front of the baby, anyway — she probably wouldn't have minded, but my mama would have had a fit — and I didn't bother calling the pool hall or the gas station. When it's long past dark and the baby's asleep, and you've got a room full of plastic parts made places you can't even pronounce, the last thing you want to know is what your man's up to. I always slept better when I didn't know.

Not that I didn't like having him around, when he was in the mood. He brought home good stuff: Mason jar of homebrew from Lenny's still, bag of weed from Sam's patch in his cornfield (what was left of it after the feds came through, anyway), new video from cousin Jack's pawnshop, bought for a couple of bucks. We'd been watching one of those the night I went into labor, something Jack had gotten off a trucker who said it'd come from Sweden. Said it was kinky stuff you couldn't do in a civilized country. Bobby cracked a beer that night and closed the drapes, and we stayed in to watch it, me swollen everywhere but my wrists, Bobby resting his can on my belly, almost blocking my view of the TV. Halfway through, around the time the chief of police was tag-teaming on the mayor's wife with his German Shepherd, one at the front door and one at the back, but before the latex convention and that thing with the fire hoses, Bobby declared this was the best porno he'd ever seen, and said we were naming our kid after the director. I checked the box, since Bobby didn't read too good — Sven Anders, it said, and Bobby liked it, said it sounded manly, but then he was drunk — still drunk when the doctor slapped our girl into the world the next day — and so she was Sven.

At least she had never had a problem sucking. Latched onto me like Bobby had done in the back of his daddy's pickup, when I still had tits instead of the teats the kid had given me.

When I finally got the parts together that night, just after the late comedian went off, and turned the damn thing on, it didn't suck at all. Instead, it blew white dust all over the room, coating the plastic parts, the carpet, the instruction booklet, and Sven, who coughed and plugged her thumb back into place. I shut it off, sat down on the coffee table, and punched the dusty couch pillows while I finished Bobby's beer, then called my daddy.

Eight o' clock the next morning, he came over with his tool kit, took one look at the back of the vacuum, and attached the final hose. Told me it wasn't a good machine, that I should never buy a Bissell, they didn't work right. I turned it on and cleaned up the powder while Sven sucked the life out of my right breast, and told him Bobby had picked it out for me.

Bobby was an idiot, Daddy said, then asked me where he'd gotten the money.

I didn't know. I didn't know anything about it until I went to get some from the bank one day and stood there as the lady behind the counter told me there was nothing left, while Sven squawked in her carrier on the floor. Nothing left, she said, and showed me exactly where it had all gone. Three thousand bucks, every bit we had put by for a new car, a bigger house, diapers — scattered. He had taken it out at weird places, ATMs in towns ten miles away, five times in one night alone. All the money, and me with the baby and the suck-blow vacuum at home, not wondering where the hell he was or what he was doing because it didn't hurt if you didn't think about it. Sven cried, and then I cried in front of God and the lady and everyone, and the bank manager took us into his office and closed the door so the other customers wouldn't have to hear.

They caught Bobby with a kilo of cocaine in his truck that afternoon.

I watched Sven's video again that night, once I'd told Bobby we didn't have anything left for his bail, but it wasn't that good the second time around. When the movie ended, I tossed the tape into the woods out the back door, then slammed it hard enough to wake the neighbors' mutt. I looked around the den until my eyes settled on the vacuum cleaner, sitting there against the wall, its clear plastic cup almost full of filth.

I wondered how much ten kilos was, if it would fill the vacuum.

Let Bobby try. I wasn't going to clean up this mess for him.

I unplugged the vacuum's hose and pushed it all over the house, watching it blow the dust it had collected, watching the dust float like glitter past the hall light, and after the cup was empty, I put it away and climbed into the bed with Sven. She found me in her sleep, mouth moving like a gasping fish, and sucked in the darkness as the fine white rain fell.

nature of theft:

I was on assignment in Columbia, South Carolina, and found myself with extra time on my hands and a rented black Mazda 6 with New York plates. After driving around the neighborhood near my hotel for a good hour, I stumbled upon the local Tuesday Morning, a discount store that had become my new best friend in my quest to furnish an apartment. I parked and wandered in, and spotted the pair of Bissell vacuums. Once I lugged one down to the register, the cashier ambled over and began to ring it up, telling me her thoughts on Bissells, how it had taken her all day to assemble hers, and how her ex-husband had been buying drugs, but that they hadn't caught him until she noticed he had taken money five times in one night from an out-of-the-way ATM. I still don't know what I did to encourage this tale, but I took my vacuum and left. Five minutes later, having learned that my sister wanted a vacuum, too, I returned and dragged the other one to the register. After spraying her hair with Lysol disinfectant to keep her curls manageable, my cashier sold me the second Bissell, and I made as hasty an exit as one can make with an upright vacuum in one's arms.

She was right – the assembly was something of a pain, especially if one neglects a hose the booklet doesn't mention and finds one's new vacuum blowing instead of sucking.

As for Sven, her name was taken from one of my friends, who has a boy's name for the same reason.

tandem

dinh vong

One day, Eileen decided she and James should take up cycling.

"It'll be fun. Something we can do together. It'll take your mind off your depression. Think about it. Whoever heard of a depressed man on a bicycle?"

"They're called clowns. I don't even remember how to ride a bicycle."

"Don't be silly. 'Like riding a bike,' people always say. It's in our neurological wiring. Muscle memory."

He hadn't wanted to. The idea was wretched. He had big plans that day. He was going to write his book, start his painting, experience his childhood traumas all over again. Instead she found him naked on the couch, watching *This Old House* with the new host he nicknamed Sparky because he was blond and full of dog-eyed pep. It was one of those mornings when, no matter how much coffee James drank, he felt lethargic, like the puppet master had let go of the strings so that he was only a lump of wood, a pile of lifeless cloth. He couldn't explain to her his depression. One day he felt tragic and brilliant, and the next he fell back inside himself. When he felt like this as a child, he would run berserk across the room, flap and dance and pirouette, fall in a huffy heap in the middle of the living room while his family watched, and told him to get out of the way of the television. But he was an adult now, so he did not. He hugged his arms and made snide comments about Sparky to no one.

"Let's ride. I miss riding. I had a boyfriend who rode. That was the only thing he ever gave me." Eileen had had many boyfriends and two husbands, and each had only given her one thing. One had given her mono. Another gave her tango lessons. Another gave her vegemite. Her last husband, Earl, had left her tremendously rich. James often feared that when the axe came, he'd be the first to leave her with nothing.

The first time they rode together, he pedaled behind her in a matching spandex suit, watching her determined thighs pump up and down. From time to time, she turned around to smile at him in her yellow plastic sunglasses and fluorescent helmet. She resembled a complicated insect. Every time another cyclist rode past, she called out "good morning," and nodded her head. James grunted, and felt bad when they did not grunt back. It began to rain, and he was relieved to see his anxiety manifested in nature. He had known in his gut there was something to mourn over.

He caught up. They rode abreast.

"This is fun," James said.

"See," Eileen said.

There was something to it, he thought, remembering that he enjoyed exercise. He felt like a bonafide living organism with blood coursing through him, through parts it may have temporarily ignored all those days he sat pooled up naked on the couch.

They saw a child in a red raincoat run up to her mother and land three great whacks on her broadside. The mother made no effort to chase the girl, who was already running away. They looked at each other and laughed. It was a rare moment when James thought how humane humanity was.

The girl distracted them, and they jostled against each other because they had been riding too close. Their handlebars clattered and stuck together. Eileen jerked her caught hand away and managed to steady herself. James wasn't so lucky and in a minute his face was on the curb. From his horizontal position, he saw Eileen jump off her bike, letting it fall with a dramatic careless crash on the sidewalk, and then run to his fallen body, screaming, "James! Sweetie! Sweetie!" and cradling his head close to her wet spandex body, smooth like a seal.

"I'm okay," he said bravely.

At home, they undressed and assessed the damage. She had an enormous blue welt on the back of her hand. He had a bloody gash on his elbow and an Alaska-shaped bruise on his thigh. "I don't feel that bad," he said. He did not tell her that at the moment of impact he had imagined his head being run over by oncoming traffic and bursting like a ripe watermelon. The image played over and over in his head like a looped movie reel.

"Wait till tomorrow," Eileen said, and poured hydrogen peroxide into his elbow wound so that it fizzled white bubbles.

James clenched his teeth together tightly. "Son of a bitch!"

The next morning his body felt like he had done a thousand push-ups, followed by a thousand sit-ups, followed by a thousand lunges. He lifted his head at the neck.

"I can't move," he said.

Eileen patted his face with her bruised hand, then got up and brought him some aspirin, disinfected his elbow and changed the bandage. While she was at work, he peeled the bandage away and picked at the dried edges of skin. He knew he shouldn't, that it would only scar, but he could never leave well enough alone. He picked and waited for the results. In the past, if he had restrained himself long enough, newly pink skin would emerge from beneath the scab, a small cause for rejoicing. This time a pool of blood formed and he had to wait all over again for it to clot and harden.

When James could walk without groaning, Eileen decided why only ride for recreation? Were the ice caps not melting? Were polar bears not swimming aimlessly towards their deaths?

"We're getting rid of the car," she said.

Eileen drove it mostly. James hated driving and didn't have a job. He had been between jobs for the last several months because of his depression. His previous job had been cashiering at a grocery co-op, and before that he had baked organic bread part-time. Money wasn't an issue because Eileen had plenty of it, and thought of work as a thing to do to keep the mind supple. James was highly aware of the convenience of Eileen's money. He minded living off the fat of her ex-husband's land. Minded and took advantage of it.

They had met in an adult-learning pottery class. James had noticed Eileen right away, because she kept looking at him as if she recognized him from somewhere. He was used to this. He had grown out his facial hair into a grizzled beard, so he resembled portraits of Christ, and was always familiar to people. He had looked back at her, though she was not his type. At the time, his type was Kristine, a mother of two, and the unofficial town whore who was proud of the title and hung red lamps outside her door in case anyone thought otherwise. Eileen looked intelligent, like a professor. Her hair was styled in an asymmetrical bob. A black sweater was thrown across her slim, narrow body, and underneath she wore a gray shift. She was like fantasies he had of librarians when he was younger. He let the edge of his mouth curl up in a flirtatious smile. He was conscious of his kind eyes that women often mistook for something deeper, and attempted to make them appear kinder by carefully controlling his facial muscles.

Later, Eileen would tell him he walked a fine line between nomad and bohemian, the kind of man she had never had the gumption to date, until now. In her late 30s, she had nothing to lose, a nice figure, and enough cash to save a man. A sensitive, artistic, lost man.

Their next ride began as a clear, bright day, so they dressed lightly — Eileen in only a T-shirt and clam diggers. But it soon became windy and cold, and globules of rain pitted dark splotches into Eileen's shirt.

"I need to buy a better shirt," she said. They locked their bikes in front of Dillard's, and then clomped into the store still wearing their cycling cleats. She tried on a sweater. Its knit pattern was angular and modern, the collar high. Wearing it, she looked like she had just flown in from the damp, wet future, with her hair clinging to the sides of her face, and the future's rain clinging to her dark hair that deflected droplets of water like dandruff or snow.

"I like it," James said. And then they were out in the rain again, fighting wind and wet, pedaling twice as hard at half the speed. The sweater was not a good choice. The wool absorbed water like a sponge and hung heavy against her. The bottom of the sweater cut away from the body so that Eileen's stomach was a block of ice when they got home. She chattered against James, pressed her cold belly against him. The gesture made him feel necessary and genuine, as if he could keep hearth fires burning. He tucked her in bed, then went to the kitchen to boil water for tea. She called out "Hurry back!" in a child's voice.

But the next day, she was well again. The muscles in her arms gave off a tan warm glow, radiating health and self-sufficiency. After that, she purchased rain slickers for both of them, and fenders for their touring bikes.

"I feel awesome," she said. She had never used that word before. "I feel young and awesome." She twirled around him on the tips of her toes. Her confidence made him afraid.

From the beginning, Eileen had been different. She had revealed herself quickly and easily, as if the woman she was now was already someone else. The most terrifying moments of her life she told him without so much as a blink:

When my mother threatened to kill herself, and shuffled through the knives in the kitchen drawer, I would hide in the clothes closet and pretend the hanging clothes were sails, and I was a Viking, heading out towards new land.

My father was a wall.

He was a funny one, Ben was. He couldn't come unless he was raping me. He would piss me off, start a huge argument, just so I wouldn't want to fuck him.

She would straddle James and bend over to embrace him so that her hair splayed out and over his chest. She would reveal her childhood, teenage, and adult abuses one by one, carefully rehearsed. All the time she had been observing him, picking him up and setting him down, seeing if her words had an effect. She had said all these things many, many times. It was like being lied to, though everything she said had really happened to her.

"Do I have an aura?" she had asked one day.

"Huh?"

"When you look at me, is there light in my eyes? Am I alive?"

"You're alive."

"No. Am I *alive*?"

"You're alive."

"Or am I like most people out there with their damn Blackberries, and ironed hair, and fake tans and tits — the living, televised dead."

James was already gone, already distracted. He should have held her face in his hands, her face with the complex and sensitive mind just beneath its surface. He should have said, "Your aura glows." Instead he shrugged his shoulders, and said, "Your tits are real." When he sensed her disappointment at his response, and felt the distance inside her becoming formidable, he grabbed her shoulders gently, and pressed her to him, cradled her head with his forearms. He was not good with words, but he had comforted women in the past with the bulk of his body.

They had settled into the routine of their relationship. There were nights when they decided to shut the doors and the blinds, and build a fort out of blankets on the couch. They watched film after film: Goddard, Buñuel, Hitchcock. They didn't speak to each other, but always made sure some part of their bodies touched, a hand or a foot pressed against the other's, a leg thrown across a lap. They dropped popcorn on the floor, emptied beer bottles and wine glasses, and when it came time to turn off the television and make love, they stumbled to the bed, kissed each other sloppily, pawed at each other, then gave up in their drunken listlessness, and fell asleep, fully clothed.

He suspected that her preoccupation with bicycles began the night they had watched *The Bicycle Thief*. When he looked over at Eileen, she was crying. He had assumed it was because she was drunk. She had said, "People are so fucking beautiful. It fucking hurts me right here," punching herself in the stomach. "Bicycles are so fucking beautiful," she said, and cried until her eyes were like shining and bloated frog bellies.

The riding became more than a diversion, more than a trip to the grocery store. Eileen began to train, as she called it. She bought dozens of books on bike maintenance and fitness. She bought *Chicken Soup for the Cyclist's Soul.* She jotted down a riding schedule in a journal and followed it religiously — 30-, 50-, even 80-mile rides. These were interspersed with rest days when she stretched and did yoga to lengthen her muscles and build core strength. She became a regular at the local bike shop. Spent thousands of dollars on a carbon fiber Cervelo, Cidi shoes, Giro helmet, bib shorts, heart rate monitor, and a power meter. She dropped $300 for some professional to shoot lasers at her knee caps while she was fitted to her bike. She drank protein and electrolyte shakes. She ate packaged blocks of glucose with flavors like Margarita and Mojito.

He could no longer keep up; she had become too fast for him, weaved through traffic like a maniac, not even pretending to wait for him. She asked if she could ride with her bike friends, which meant she would no longer be riding with him. She signed up for group rides and was gone most mornings with other racers she had met at the shop. Women *and* men.

There was one, Carlos, who called late one night. James picked up the phone and was startled to hear a man's voice asking for Eileen.

"Who the fuck is this?" James said.

"Who is it?" Eileen said, fear in her voice.

The man on the phone said, "Calm down, dud. Dud, I'm Carlos. Eileen's riding buddy." Since when did Eileen spend time with people who said "dude"? He had a

Cuban accent and James imagined him dark, lean, muscular, with a firm ass and powerful thighs.

"Don't call my wife after eleven, motherfucker."

"Who is that?" Eileen asked, and before he could hang up, wrestled the phone out of his hand. When she found out it was Carlos, she apologized effusively.

"No, don't blame your — no Carlos — he's depressed — not acting like himself. It's no problem. Don't worry. I'll see you in the morning. At six." And after she hung up, her ingratiating voice turned steely.

"Since when have I become your wife?" she screamed, and hurled the phone at him.

The more she became involved with her new group of friends, the more sex wasn't enough. When they made love, he found himself thrusting harder and deeper inside of her, holding himself there for long intervals, trying to stave off coming for as long as he could as she shifted uncomfortably beneath him, growing bored, he suspected. James wanted to open Eileen's body along an invisible seam and crawl inside of her. She didn't look him in the eyes anymore. Instead of talking in the morning, she studied the back of the cereal box, chewing silently.

She began offering their home every Friday night for DVD viewings of any film that was bike themed. The group would watch the Tour de France, Giro d'Italia, *Breaking Away*. One night it was *The Triplets of Belleville*. Their living room was full, so James sat at the back against the baseboards that he had never really noticed before. He wondered if Earl painted these when he and Eileen were still together and immediately felt jealous. This was another man's house, another man's baseboards.

Did the demise of Eileen and Earl begin much like this, with a new hobby? He looked over at Eileen, who had a good seat on the couch, and was surrounded by her new friends. She was sitting like a child, with her knees tucked up to her chest, and her arms around her legs. He watched her eyes lighting up with the French film, nonsense as far as he could tell. There were no words, only animation and music. Three enormously fat sisters tried to catch frogs in pots, and the group laughed as if they understood it. Eileen seemed miles away over the sea of heads. At the funniest parts of the movie, she turned to Carlos to see if he was laughing too, so that they could laugh together.

For his birthday a few weeks before, she had bought James a tandem bicycle. On the card she had written that it was symbolic of their journey through life together. But she had never asked him to ride it with her. It only took up space, leaning against the wall in the hallway. *Symbolic*, he thought bitterly.

He knew now he had been wrong about Eileen. There was nothing about her to feel sorry over. She chose and discarded her insane, abusive men. She had chosen him at his most disheveled state, brought him home to her bed, civilized him, until he was like domesticated livestock — slow, dim-witted, and moving towards the fearful, irrevocable future.

It had all been a bad idea, this woman, with her wealth and endless hobbies. Sure, James had been betrayed before by other women. He had even stumbled in on Kristine with another man, and shut the door so he wouldn't disturb them. But he had expected something different from Eileen. Something bookish and classy.

He wanted to wipe away the entire room with his hand. He brought his own knees to his chest, and rested his forehead on his knees. He closed his eyes and saw a memory of Eileen, so different from who she was now. He saw her emerging from the bathroom, hair falling softly around her face, the rims of her eyes gleaming. She looked like a half-sleeping child. She came up to him, pinched his cheek, and said, "You're stinky."

He lifted his head, and looked at Eileen again. She was reaching into the popcorn bowl at the same time as Carlos, so that their hands touched. He raged silently. He found himself wanting to be one of the people who had hardened her, who had known all her stories at the time when she still told them with tears, how her father was a wall. As it was, if he said, "I love you," she would laugh at his naïveté. And if he said, "I hate you," she'd say, "You weren't the first and you certainly won't be the last." She loved him with the passion of a pet owner growing weary of his habits. He could never really devastate her. All those entrances into her heart had closed like a vacuum-sealed sweater bag that his love glanced easily off.

The next morning was Saturday, grocery day. Eileen would be gone all morning on one of her rides, so James sat down to write out a grocery list:

Bread
Milk
Tea
Eggs

The list comforted him. Made him feel like his needs were simple. He had never asked for much. Since the car was sold, he would need to ride his bike to get groceries.

He hooked the panniers on to the rear rack, made sure he brought his head- and taillights even though the day was bright and blinding. He picked up the checkbook, which was behind the lucky cat statue on the credenza. They were Eileen's checks, but the grocer knew them both and never gave James problems. And Eileen was trusting. She had come to the money easily and threw it away just as easily, never keeping track of missing checks or her bank book left lying wide open on the kitchen table. She had no reason to worry. James was no thief.

He tucked the list and checkbook into his back pocket and stared thoughtfully for a while at the lucky cat's benign grin. Then he took out a scrap of paper, wrote down her account number and passwords, which were all written neatly in the bank book because Eileen couldn't be bothered with remembering things. He returned the checkbook back behind the cat.

He imagined that when Eileen had figured out what happened — that James had disappeared, and that thirty grand was missing from her account — she would confide in Carlos. Carlos would hold her as she sobbed, and later, they would make use of his muscular legs and ass. In the morning, delighted with their newfound love, they would ride the tandem to The Breakfast Depot, ringing their bells for the fun of it.

The image made James cry a little. He loved Eileen, even as he was robbing her.

He switched the panniers to the tandem bike, left his own bike leaning in the hallway, his bike that was too large to ever fit Carlos. He took one last look at the house, then pedaled out into the driveway, and onto the low-traffic side streets that he and Eileen had become so familiar with, dragging the weight of the empty seat behind him.

nature of theft:

This story was stolen from a bike shop owner a year ago when I noticed a tandem bike sitting in a corner of the shop, and was looking at it. He told me a married couple had purchased the bike because the wife had recently come into a lot of money and wanted to buy a celebration gift. They never picked the bike up because the husband ended up running away to Mexico with all his wife's money. The image of the tandem bike sitting in the bike store with this terrible history behind it resonated with me, and I created this story from it.

not even an ambulance can save you

jo swingler

I'm a little surprised when I see the ambulance outside Nan's house. She was alright when I popped in for breakfast on the way to school this morning, and she's tough as old boots, is Nan, so she can't have had an accident or anything like that. She used to be a nurse. She doesn't do accidents. So why's there an ambulance? I ring the bell and there's Nan right at the door. She's got her best pinny on, so it must be visitors.

"Claire," she says, all posh. "Come in. We're just having a cup of tea and the Brothers were saying how they'd love to meet you."

"Oh," I say, cos I have no idea what she's on about. What brothers? I haven't got any brothers. Her brothers? None of them live round here. I wonder a bit on the doorstep, but I go in anyway. I'm directed towards the Best Front Room, so it's definitely visitors. I look at Nan to see if there's anything in her face that'll tell me who it is, but there isn't. So there's no choice but to go in.

There's four of them. Three squashed in together on the best settee; all knees-bent-up and socks revealed. Sandals. The other one's on the armchair by the gas fire. The Good Chair. Used to be granddad's but now it's reserved for honoured guests. I look at them. These men in dresses and brown. Why are there monks in me Nan's front room? Monks? On a Wednesday? I don't know where to start. What's the protocol? Maybe I should curtsey like I have to at Mass in front of the altar. Or maybe that's just too bizarre. What's the collective noun for monks? A blessing? A communion? I dunno. There's space where there should be words.

"Claire," says Nan, wafting me further into the room to stand bottle-green in me school uniform amongst the Brothers, "say good afternoon."

"Good afternoon," I say and smile as best I can, but I can feel me face doing something unholy. So I take me hat off. Scrunch it up into me hand.

"G'day, Claire," says the one in the armchair, "Mrs Farrell has been telling us all manner of worthy things about yourself. It's a pleasure to finally meet you." And he grins. There are freckles. So many freckles all over his face, joining up into something that could be a representation of something else. But I'm too scared to look for long enough to figure it out. We don't get sun like that in Brum. Not enough for freckles.

But I smile again. It's the best way. It still hasn't been explained why there are four monks in me Nan's front room of a Wednesday afternoon. Four monks from Australia. Four Australian monks drinking English tea and sitting on me Nan's best settee, monks who possibly have a connection to the ambulance parked so blatantly outside. So I'm treading warily here, I'm treading warily till I get the bigger picture. This is unusual. Even for Nan.

Then me Nan goes, "Claire, they've come all the way from Melbourne, you know." And looks at me in a way that suggests I should've known this.

"Oh," I say.

The monks collectively lean forward. There's an air of expectancy, breaths held in anticipation. One of the monks leans forwards further than all the others and scratches at his ankle underneath the elastic top of his sock and the sound of it fills the room. Scrape scrape scrape it goes and I see a tiny cloud of dead white skin flake into the air around his lower leg. I watch. I watch some more. Scrape scrape scrape he goes and bits of him falling off onto me Nan's clean carpet. Holy skin though. The holy dead skin of a monk.

"Claire, dear," me Nan says, and it's like a dig in the ribs.

I pull myself back from the cloud of dead monk-skin and try and think of something sensible to say.

"So, the ambulance? Is that… ?"

"Yeah, too right it is," says the freckled one in the armchair. "The best thing ever for travelling."

The flaky skinned one joins in, "Yeah, we picked it up off some fella yer cousin knows. Cousin Pat. Patrick. He sorted it out fer us while we were on the boat."

"Six weeks," says the one wedged in the middle. The littlest. But the one with the biggest beard. The biggest beard I've ever seen. It's bigger than his face. Seems to be taking it over, taking over his whole face. Perhaps it's his offering to Jesus and His Sacrifice. A bearded offering. An offering of hair and itchiness. His own hair shirt but facial. And not a shirt.

"Six weeks?" I eventually manage.

The one in the armchair nods. Eyes all wide. Freckles blurring together. "Yeah, six weeks on a boat. It was amazing." And he makes his hands do this thing like it's the world. Like it's the whole world. The whole world stretched thin over the *maaaay* of amazing. And he looks dead excited with his eyes all big and shiny.

"Yer Nan did it, too, ya know?" says the one on the right hand side of the settee. He doesn't have a beard, but looking at his chin, I think he probably should. Then his eyes go all wide, too, and I think he probably shouldn't have talked about me Nan like that. But I actually like that he has. He looks down at his hands with the rosary knotted there. I can see his lips move.

I turn towards me Nan and grin. There's something about their accent that's kind of getting to me — the ease of it. I want to speak that way too. I want to be Aussie and not Brummy no more. Me Nan's Irish, so she's sorted really. She doesn't have much of a choice in it. But I hate being Brummy. It's not fair I was born here. It's really not. "Did you?" I say, staring at her, and it comes out much meaner than I'd like and I feel I have to deflect the monkly gaze and so I soften it to, "Yes, you went all the way to Oz, didn't you? It must've been… " but I'm stuck for an adjective and so I stop.

"Yes." She says. All nursely. "I did. And you well know it."

She folds her arms and looks at all the monks in a sort of holy challenge, and they all look down at their sandals and nod.

"All the way to Orange," says flaky-skin.

I don't know where Orange is. But I see in my head a place like an orange, and maybe that's the colour of Australia.

"Yer Cousin Pat was there to wave her off," says Armchair.

And they all look at me as if the Black Marks are on my Soul for not being there to wave me Nan off on her six-week voyage to see her sisters and brothers on the other side of the world. A journey she hated and a journey I wasn't old enough to see. No, not even not old enough. Not alive enough. But somehow it's still some kind of sin on my part. A sin of omission. Not being born and therefore missing me Nan heading off on her epic journey to see her brothers and sisters all the way over in Australia is a Sin. It's my fault. I want to cross-off being Catholic as well as Brummy. But as soon as that thought leaps into me head, me Catholic Conscience is beating it down, beating it down, beating it back into the Fiery Pits of Hell Where It Belongs. The monks are watching. The Black Marks are etching themselves ever more deeply into my Soul. I can feel them blackening in. Monks' eyes. God's vessels. Monks. They can see. There's too much holiness here. I'm not sure I can deal with it. It's like…

"Claire," says Nan. Eyes. Teeth. False, yes, but meaningful. There's meaning in those teeth. Yet I'm still no clearer. It's all just Sin and Avenging Angels in my head. I probably need to say something now. Join in. Be part of it. But be a part of what? I think I need to sit down.

"The ambulance?" I say, but it's not really speaking, it's more of a sigh and a gesture to the window, where the brightness of the ambulance is resting — lurking on the other side of the glass.

"Yeah," says the one who hasn't spoken yet. "Yeah," he says again, but it's just some drawling slur. Is that Godly? He's very young, so maybe he hasn't got the hang of all of this monkliness yet. "So the ambulance?" he says and it's a question. The way he says it it's like a question but how am I supposed to answer?

"Yeah," he says again. "The ambulance is beaut. It's got loads of room."

"Tonnes," says beardy.

"Wanna see?" says the freckly one.

And I can feel me Nan crossing her arms tight across her bosom and not wishing this to happen. Her pinny crackles with her disapproval. So I look around the room at these men and their brown-ness brightened up with their joy and I go, "Yes, love to."

Outside, having squeezed past Nan's annoyance, we're standing at the back of the ambulance. Beardy and Freckles are giggling about with the lock on the rear swing-open doors and it's like watching babbies. This is all madness for them. I stand on the pavement in me Nan's sensible street and feel the weight of neighbourly nosiness pressing in and the heavier it gets, the longer I want this ambulance to be here. The Black Marks are etching in again but this time I'm ignoring them. I watch the swing doors do their thing.

"So," says Beardy, "here we go." And he waves his hand at the darkened space where usually there is blood and almost-deadness and injuries and pain. I lean in to look. Instead of bodies, there are four neat bunks where the stretchers ought to be. Four neat hospital-cornered bunks with a little pillow at the driver's end of each. Four male faces gleam. "Isn't it the best?" says one. I can't take in who. I just look at the beds and think… what?

Sandaled feet scuffle then there's a rush of brown and one of them's jumped in. Leapt right in with a flourish. It's the young, less-monkly one. He's grinning and saying stuff about how lovely it all is and how convenient and how Uncle Pat's friend's done them proud and the ease of travelling about in this ambulance is something to behold. And how much it means to them to be seeing the family. The British ones.

I look towards the front door, where Nan is standing. Pinny rigid to deflect the gaze of neighbours. But she knows it's not enough. There's nothing can stave off their desire to know.

"Family?" I say.

"Yeah, we're off round the country visiting the Brit side of your family," says the young one, from the depths of the ambulance. "Too expensive by train, so we've got this." And he smacks his hand on the inside wall of the ambulance and it makes a metallic thud.

Beardy starts counting off on his fingers, "There's yer cousins, Pat, John and David. Yer great-aunts Beattie, Sissy and Maggie. They're in Devon. There's yer Cousin Claire and Big Claire and Auntie Annie… and finally there's yer mum, Eileen." And he grins at me, triumphant.

No! I yell. In my head. Please don't go and see me

Mom. Not me Mom. Not there. Not in our house. You can't. I look round at me Nan, still guarding the doorway, and there's a flicker across her face that tells me she's thinking the same. I don't know what to do, what to say. I wait for Nan to sort something.

"She's not well, I'm afraid," she says. "She's ever so poorly, is Eileen, and it's probably best she doesn't have visitors for a while. Claire, here, bless her, has been so good with the looking after of her mother. Haven't you love?"

And she looks at me and I make my face go into something that looks sad and pitiful and distressed by it all. Looking after me poorly Mom, it's hard on a girl my age. And the monks all look at me and I'm sure they can tell what the truth is, but how could they? Unless there's something divine and interventiony going on, but I'm sure even God couldn't be doing with that. Not just now, anyway.

"Ah, well," says the freckled one. "Can't be helped. God has his ways, and who are we to question them. Least we've met you, Claire. And I'm sure you'll pass our blessings on to your mother." And he smiles really nicely at me and I just feel the Black Marks cutting in again cos of all these lies. But I smile nicely back and mumble something in agreement. And all four of the monks look at me in sympathetic ways and I'm not sure I can cope with all this holiness directed right at me like that. Burning, almost. Nan! I shout, in my head. And she hears, she must do, cos she starts saying things about tea and sandwiches and how they'd probably like to be getting on soon, what with all the travelling they have ahead of them, and all the cousins and sisters and people to be seeing around here. And wouldn't they like a drop of tea before they go? And they all nod their heads and say yes that would be lovely and how kind of her to be looking after them so well, and English tea is the best. So we all mooch back into the house and lock out the nosy neighbours and lock out the lies and it's just the six of us with cups of tea and bread and dripping and Spam sandwiches and it's good.

And then they're going. Three of them packed into the back of the ambulance and the beardy one in the driving seat. But they don't ring the bell cos it's been de-clappered, which is a shame, I think. So there's waving and blessings and messages to be passed on and then, in a scramble, they're off. I watch the squatting whiteness of the ambulance hug its way round the corner and imagine the larks and laughs of the monks as they bounce about inside. And once they've gone, I kiss me Nan on her downy, soft cheek and say ta-rah. She pushes closed the big front door and then I head back to Mom's. To the guzzunda, almost overflowing, stinking of piss and worse. To the sink full of unclean dishes. To the bottles stashed where she thinks I can't find them. I head back. But she'll still be in bed, so I'll have a bit of time to myself before she staggers up, wanting gin from the out-door and chips. And I think about the existence of somewhere new at the end of six weeks at sea. I think about the monks travelling about the country in an ambulance seeing family. My family. I think about all of that and tuck it away to keep just for meself. Cos that'll do for now. That'll just have to do.

nature of theft:

This is stolen from my mum, the 'Claire' of the story. She mentioned once to me about going to see her Nan, must have been sometime in the 60s, and arriving to find four monks sitting in the front room. They'd been travelling around the country in the back of ambulance and had come from Australia to visit the English branch of her extended family. The family was Irish and lots of the brothers and sisters (my great, great aunts and uncles) had left Dublin and emigrated to Australia. I have no idea who the monks were, neither does my mum. I have no more details, other than that fragment of my mum's memory; four monks in the back of an ambulance at her Nan's.

the death queue

regi claire

The first time your daughter phoned was three weeks ago, late morning. You'd once told me she didn't trust me, had never trusted any of your women friends, but not to worry: Claudia was grown-up now and your affairs were none of her business.

This was different. "An emergency," she said, and there were tears in her voice. "They found him unconscious on the office floor, Diva wouldn't stop barking and whimpering. Now he's in intensive care." She sniffed, blew her nose. "Lung cancer. Inoperable. I thought you might... "

I didn't wait to hear the rest. Sharp-edged things knocked into me as I gasped my way towards the window. My mouth had torn open to suck in the air, all the air in the room, the flat, the building. My lungs filled with dank shreds of autumn fog as I hung over the windowsill in the oversized sweatshirt I wear now that I hardly leave the house anymore. Whole convoys of lorries might have thundered past on the street below, flashing their lights, whole brigades of shoppers with staring eyes and clanging tins, jars and bottles, pavementfuls of shrill clattering schoolchildren — what the hell did I care.

Once I'd recovered myself and retrieved the phone from the floor, the line was dead. I decided to write to her instead. Dug out some notepaper from under a pile of glossy old theatre programmes and take-away menus in a drawer I still haven't had the energy to clear out so others won't have to, later.

19 October, noon, Flat 3, Zürcherstrasse 7A I put in my usual left-handed spider-sprawl, then paused. Fancy me, of all people, feeling the need to pinpoint my coordinates in time and space!

Dear Claudia — I paused again. I hate writing things, especially letters. And the girl's a virtual stranger, even if she *is* your daughter. The sleeve of my sweatshirt had smeared her name, but I couldn't bear starting over. She'd assume I'd been crying, which I suppose I was, in a dry, inside sort of way. I continued, quickly now, to be done with it:

I'm terribly sorry about your father... Adrian has always seemed so fit and well, going for runs with Diva, playing squash, tennis, badminton. There was no sign of anything wrong with him the last time we met, in summer. And he never complained, never said a word about being in pain.

I stopped myself from adding: *Surely, this is a mistake. Because it should have been me, not him. I'm the one that's ill, has been ill for years. Not him. I'm the one that's supposed to be dying, for God's sake!*

In the end I scrawled *You're in my thoughts, and so is Adrian. Poor dear Adrian...* And rushed off to the bathroom. My nose had started bleeding again. As I crouched and retched into the toilet bowl, I could feel the brittleness of my left jaw, my teeth rattling like gravel, so loose now, so frighteningly loose.

Then came her voicemail message on Tuesday night.

I'd been having one of my mammoth phone sessions: two-and-a-half fluid hours of vodka (an excellent painkiller) and chat with Jenny, at twenty-four one of my youngest friends. You were always amazed (or is 'envious' more to the point?) that most of my closest friends are half my age. Is this maybe the secret of eternal youth: not creams or peels or plastic surgery, but the sheer openness of allowing one's younger self to be alive and laugh and cry along with the young? Anyway, Jenny had been accused of 'carrying on' with a seventeen-year-old pupil from her French class ("A real hunk of jailbait, and no innocent," she described him, leering audibly) and needed a bit of advice on how to straighten matters out with the school board.

Before listening to my messages, I got myself another refill on the rocks and collapsed into the chintzy sofa, one of the few relics salvaged from my first marriage. I was suddenly exhausted. My hands were shaking so much the slim strips of maroon polish down the middle of my nails seemed to writhe and multiply. Christ, I used to be able to stay up till all hours, looking good, flirting and holding my drink, but this new round of chemo is getting to me — I seem to shrink overnight and wake up sad and bleeding, my mouth clogged with disgust. I swigged some vodka to rid myself of the taste that's with me now at all times, the taste of my own decay, then punched the 'Play' button.

And there was her message, a wavering blur of sobs: "It's Claudia here. Please call me." To be honest, I hesitated for a minute or two, drank down the entire glass to prepare myself for what I'd already guessed was coming.

Why not me? I couldn't help thinking, *Why do others get to jump the death queue, and not me?* Almost immediately, of course, I felt guilty. Ashamed of myself. The large papery fronds of my indoor palm tree rustled their reproach in the faint draught from the hall, and I shivered. It had been a windy afternoon, cold, with the occasional flurry of bright gritty rain pinging off the window panes and dead leaves scraping and scuttling across the concrete of the balcony floor. The alcohol I'd consumed that evening, the only 'food' my stomach appears to accept without complaint these days, had made my eyes water. I wanted nothing more than to crawl into a corner of my sofa and hide myself there like a cat, for no one to find and stroke back to life.

Claudia just cried for a while and I sat listening, crumpled into my corner, eyes closed, doing my best not to let go of the phone. When she finally managed to tell me you had died on Sunday without regaining consciousness, I felt genuinely happy for you. You'd have hated being dependent. Remember what you said that weekend in April? *Let's agree on a buffer zone where we can meet without trespassing, without inflicting or committing ourselves.* Pure legalese and at first I'd screamed at you, I was so bloody furious. Remember how in answer you took my hands, quietly turned them over and, one by one, kissed the soft pads of my fingers? Something inside me flipped over then, and I smiled against my will. But there won't be any more buffer zones now. Only a place in my memory that will always be ours.

Claudia started sniffling again. "The cremation is on Thursday. You're very welcome."

I swallowed hard and stared over at the rustling palm fronds as if they could soothe away the sudden queasiness I felt.

"I don't think that would be a good idea, Claudia," I said at last. "I'll be paying my respects in private, here."

Perhaps I imagined it, but her "I understand" sounded relieved. She'll never trust me now, I know. Then she said, in an odd, flinty tone: "I almost forgot, he's left something for you" — and I realised she was jealous.

Can you picture it? Your healthy young daughter jealous of me, a middle-aged woman with a tired, disintegrating body that's become a battlefield for surgeons? (The consolation is that the growths can't go much further, now they've reached my head.)

For a moment I remained silent, wondered what on earth you could have possibly wanted me to have. My weight in gold, maybe? (I could do with that.)

"Father's associate will bring it round, Karl von Arp — he suggested it, actually."

I ignored her unspoken question. I could have told her, *Yeah, you're right: Karl and I have always had a soft spot for each other, but nothing's ever happened. Because of your father. Satisfied?* Brushing it all aside, I said, "That's very nice of him. Any time is fine. As long as it's evenings." My feeble joke fell on stony ground, as expected, and we finished soon afterwards.

No one appeared the following evening. Instead Jürgen rang, the features editor of *World Week* (and a former lover, why not admit it). He persuaded me to do some more proofreading for him, no doubt to bolster my sagging bank balance, and perhaps my self-esteem. "Flexi-time," he coaxed, "plus you work from home. I'll drop off a laptop and get you onto the net, sweet as a kiss." How could I refuse? And I was rather looking forward to seeing him.

I'd barely replenished my glass and buttered a slice of white bread, soft and crustless to minimise the pain of chewing, when the phone went again: Floriano, my ex-brother-in-law. Regaling me with tales of his mother's senile dementia — that afternoon, she'd apparently mistaken his pocket radio for a hamster and insisted on feeding it. And so on and so on.

My third caller was Jane, minutes later.

"Oh," she said, "you're quick. So desperate you're waiting by the phone now? Only kidding!"

I laughed, sipped more drink.

Sad old Jane. Sharp as a broken needle. You'd met her twice, and didn't like her. 'Maladjusted' and 'neurotic' were some of your kinder remarks. I just feel sorry for her. Pale, beautiful Jane who went through primary school half-starved because her parents had a dozen kids and no money — until they were catapulted into riches-ville after her father won the lottery.

And now her newest husband has been diagnosed with prostate cancer... "Perhaps he fucked about too much when he was young," she blurted out. "Least, that's what I heard on the radio recently: too many partners from too young."

All at once I'd had it. Why do people always choose *me*, for Christ's sake? Turning me into some bloody confessor figure, asking me for absolution of what — their own callousness? "Sorry, Jane," I almost shouted, "but that's not *my* problem. You want to discuss it, go and see his doctor. Ciao," and, reaching down for the phone plug, I slipped it out of the socket, smooth as anything. I was surprised at myself, and pleased. Peace at last.

I kept the phone unplugged throughout Thursday. Even while I was out at the shops for a fresh bottle of vodka, some French Brie and tomatoes. Then at the doctor's to have my pharynx drained, a disgusting thrice-weekly necessity I'll never get used to, let alone be able to perform myself, not in this life, at any rate. All that stinking slime, that sludge... Do you remember how one night in a moment of grandiose passion — love conquers all, that kind of stuff — you'd vowed you would do it for me? And how, once acquainted with the finer details, you convincingly argued your way out of the job? You were never one for the grim physicalities of existence, were you, Adrian? As darkness fell and the wind picked up again, howling as if in agony, slapping my windows with wet teary drops, I knew you'd passed through the fire, or the fire through you. And you were truly gone.

Next evening Karl turned up with a plastic bag, a chilled bottle of Bollinger and a sad, forced smile that made the thick tendons in his throat strain like ropes. He was ten minutes early, but I was ready for him. Thank God I'd had the sense to reconnect the phone. There'd even been time for a quick bath and change, a mouthwash and several generous squirts of Opium.

I'd forgotten how burly he was (in Jenny-speak definitely another 'real hunk') and must have gaped at him as he stood looking at me, his lavender eyes skimming over my black dress (my favourite because its cut gives the illusion of curves), then lingering on my face. On my hair — which is still my own. Still down to my shoulders, wheat blonde and frizzy. My one pride and joy, and a token of how much I've suffered. Worth the most paralysing arctic cold from that ice blue chemo cap, worth the most punishing headaches.

"Your hair is beautiful," he said eventually and, setting down the carrier bag and the champagne on the hall floor, he folded me in his arms as if I was breakable.

I pressed myself against him to prove I did have some strength left. I could feel his big body slump a little, then begin to tremble. For a long moment we held on to each other, clinging, trembling together, dancing our slow swaying dance of loss.

"Poor you," he whispered after a while, a little ambiguously, before adding, "Adrian was such a good man. Any tricky case, and he'd be there to guide me through the legal maze."

Rubbing my head on the shoulder of his soft wool jacket, I breathed in his smell, a mixture of cigarette smoke, faded aftershave, deodorant, and pure male muskiness — in the last few years I've become an expert at identifying bodily odours.

"You know," he continued, "what bothers me is that Adrian never once mentioned feeling unwell. Though the doctors believe he must have been in severe pain." He lifted my chin carefully with one hand. "Did he ever say anything to you?"

I shook my head, not quite trusting my voice, and closed my eyes so he wouldn't see... what? My confusion? My disappointment at confidences unshared? Or self-pity, naked and ugly? I caught myself sneaking a glance at the plastic bag and speculating about your bequest.

After Karl had opened the Bollinger, easing out the cork with the softest of pops, we chinked glasses. "Well, cheers!" he said, then suddenly checked himself. Started blinking, "That's what *he*'d have wanted us to do, no?"

I nodded and wedged myself deeper into the corner of the sofa, legs tucked safely underneath (the idea of sitting with my feet dangling free, two inches off the floor, seemed too daunting). The black fabric of my dress lay creased around my knees, but I resisted the urge to pat it down and drank the champagne in quick, searing sips.

Karl had been watching me and now leant back in his armchair, his left hand brushing over his darkened eyes. He sounded husky when he spoke: "I don't blame you for not going to the funeral yesterday... " Again his hand strayed near his eyes.

"Well, chances are I'll be at the next one." I gave a short laugh and tossed my hair, trying to convince myself it's better to die with laughter lines than etchings of grief. Have a dance, come on, an inner voice prompted me — I wondered for a second whether that could have been *you*? Then I heard myself say it out loud: "Let's dance," and I flushed at my recklessness.

Without waiting for a reply I slid off the sofa and swished past the palm fronds, leaving them bobbing and fluttering like a group of flustered heads. Something sharp and rappy, I kept thinking, sharp and rappy, as I bent over the sound system squeezed between the CDs on my wall-to-wall brick-and-board bookshelf. My eyes flicked from Bach, Beethoven and Brahms to The Beatles, from Dvořák to Marlene Dietrich to Dire Straits. Karl's ominous silence unnerved me and I grabbed one, fumbled the disc into the machine and pressed Play.

"Break On Through" boomed out of the speakers. My spine tingled at the eerie appropriateness of that song. *Weird Scenes Inside the Gold Mine* by The Doors, plucked from the shelf blindly, it seemed. Smiling, I swung round to Karl, in time to the beat: "How about this for starters?"

But he sat frowning at me as if I'd gone crazy. After an endless pause he looked away, brought out a packet of Marlboros and, still frowning, started to tap one loose, then abruptly squashed it between his fingers, dropping the crumbly remains on the coffee table. "Sorry," he mouthed and poured himself more champagne. Gulped it in one. Coughed. And snatched up the plastic bag he'd placed beside his chair, as if in a hurry to get things over with, and get away.

"Please," I said, "not now. Later." I went and took him

by the hand, pulled. "Please, Karl."

At some point during "Love Street" he mumbled into my ear that I was like a ballerina, just as delicate. That all he wanted was to put me in his pocket and carry me around with him, always. By then, of course, we'd had the Bollinger and were well into a bottle of Rioja.

I waited to open the bag until Karl had driven off. My nose felt swollen again and I hoped to God it wouldn't start bleeding. "Three hours at most," the doctor in Emergency had warned me, ten days ago. "If it doesn't stop by itself within three hours, you have to come here." There was no need for him to make his meaning plain, I could guess the 'or else'.

A box. A battered-looking, splotchy grey shoebox tied with string and knotted. *Men's Boots*, a small label said at the side, *size 11*, *black*. On the lid was my name, printed in crimson, your handwriting unmistakable.

I cut the string with the kitchen scissors and found — not ashes, but letters. Yours to me: never-sent fragments of beginnings, of half-pages and pages, many of them marred by heavily scored-out words and phrases, most breaking off in mid-sentence, and each and every one unsigned, bearing witness to your lawyerly scruples.

Dearest,

the most recent bit-page read (dated 12 August),

I've vowed to finish and post this epistle, if only to prove to myself I can still manage my own affairs (!)

~~without recourse to~~ the help of a secretary. ~~Let me say how much I loved~~ I really enjoyed being with you last weekend. How ~~blissful~~ wonderful if we could spend a few days over New Year together. What do you ~~think~~ say? Karl has told me about a nice charming little hotel near the mountains where he stayed in spring. Very discreet and rather comfortable according to him (they offer breakfast in bed so you wouldn't have to get up). Or we could go ~~wherever you like~~

— And there your pen or patience ran out. Odd you never actually talked to me about this. And now it will never happen.

The shoebox also contained a handful of letters I'd written to you, and I threw them out at once — they were yours.

Then came the photos. Photos I had no notion existed, of us both, snapped on the sly because God knows (and you certainly did!) that I'd have refused to pose for them. I glanced through the pile, feeling slightly sick, almost dizzy, despite another painkiller.

The pictures had mainly been taken in restaurants (easy to slip a waiter a tip and the camera, yes?). The only one I've decided to keep is from some boat trip I can't even remember, with the wind whipping the hair around our faces.

The rest of the box seemed filled with decorations, menus and place settings from parties we'd been invited to; your name writing itself over and over again before my eyes until it was a blur of curves and straights and slashes, totally lost in the midst of glitter-wrapped sweets, tiny umbrellas from sundaes or long drinks, and ancient chocolate hearts.

Underneath it all were layers and layers of paper napkins. What a hoarder you were! At least that's what I thought at first. But when I seized the topmost, several pressed flowers fell out — slightly faded yet recognisably gentians and edelweiss. The next one revealed two nearly black rapunzel-rampions and a Venus's slipper. I've now laid them out on my coffee table — all the flowers you ever gathered during our walks. Or rather *your* walks with and without Diva, while I relaxed in cafés and restaurants. The gentians were still a deep summer-sky blue...

I do remember *that* trip. Going up the mountains in a cable car and the slack lurch in the pit of my stomach, that split-second's free fall every time we passed a support pillar. And later the gourmet lunch at the hotel, then me in a deckchair on the sun-drenched terrace, a book and a half-bottle of wine for company while you went off hiking. How irritated you were to find me, on your return, in the very same place, laughing and squinting up at you in the brightness of the afternoon, the empty bottle raised in welcome.

Sitting here now, I toast my former self on that hotel terrace in the Alps and see my reflection stare back at me from the polished crystal of my glass of Rioja. The skin's stretched tight, the eyes are pools of darkness, the cheekbones curved to distortion, and everything's mottled by the rustling shadows of the palm fronds.

Two weeks. Two weeks was all it took you to die.

Slowly the reflection begins to disappear as I watch, and wait.

nature of theft:

This is, in many ways, the story of my best friend, Ruth, in Switzerland. It was pieced together and became part of my imagination over the course of many long-distance phone calls with her.

Ruth was diagnosed with cancer more than twenty years ago, when the doctors gave her maybe a year to live. Although close to death for a long time, she only ever talked about her illness if asked outright. At most she'd make little asides about the indignities of her daily life, casual and unsentimental, often very funny — she loves having a good laugh. She'd regale me with stories about herself and her many friends and acquaintances (at one point, for example, she met Fellini and his Swiss lover at a house party thrown by the Zurich publisher she then worked for).

What has always annoyed her is the way some people use her as a confessor figure whenever they find themselves touched by tragedy, as if her own suffering has somehow made her immune to that of others. Probably hardest for her to come to terms with have been the deaths of several friends and relatives who fell ill, then died and were 'at peace'. One of them was N. (Adrian in my story), a fitness-freak former lover of hers, whose sudden death of lung cancer within the space of only two weeks threw into such stark relief her own, unbearably long-drawn-out 'waiting'. And yes, that shoebox really 'existed'.

As you can guess from my use of the present tense, Ruth is still alive. She was recently, quite miraculously, declared 'cancer-free', thanks to advances in modern medicine.

story

louis e. bourgeois

Marcel often went without food or sleep for five days in a row, in which he could say, with full confidence, that he was being considerate about not waking the sun. This is to say, he often crossed his Rubicon, perhaps up to twenty times a year. Victor, however, was not impressed with Marcel's excessive attempts at becoming the greatest writer to ever live. On the other hand, Marcel was not in the business of impressing Victor, whom he didn't even like. But Victor wouldn't go away, not unlike a couple of Marcel's ex-girlfriends. Marcel cared little for anyone except Marcel, Nietzsche, Macbeth and Napoleon, in that order.

Victor and Marcel were often accustomed to sitting on the floor and playing jacks, because Victor paid his half of the rent on time and wouldn't go away. In the den, a sword glistened in the corner, many cacti stood solemn forming a simple motif, diplomas of English and Philosophy hung in victory. Hours departed, bread molded, beer went flat, and dialogue was sometimes exchanged on the floor:

V: Do you think it should be real toads in imaginary gardens, or vice versa?

M: I completely refuse to speak metaphysically.

V: What will they say of you when you die?

M: That his pursuit was not new.

V: That's very uncreative.

M: One is not master of one's mind with a full gut and after a long nap.

V: Do you think it a little extreme to prohibit the carrying of flowers into the garden?

Their lives were filled with incongruent transitions. For instance, it was during one of these normal conversations that an incredible knock was heard at the door. It was to Marcel's surprise that the city's quail hunter was standing at the door holding an enormous drum fish. What didn't make sense was that Marcel sent the quail hunter on an outing to buy cigarettes. No logical connection could be made, so Victor called a local prostitute to make an exchange for the gray-eyed drum fish.

Marcel wanted to write verse that was self-implosive (destructive). He had come really close to doing this with the utmost velocity of evil, but every time he was about to break through, Kora or Javalia would come over (Kora, often with a blue guitar, Javalia with forceful lessons in psychology) and throw his verse back into clonal achievements of the past. Marcel thought and thought and thought and thought a lot about what to do, and finally he decided to take a train to Jackson, Mississippi, and try his hand at prose. The end result was very saddening and when Marcel got back from Jackson, Victor was forced to read this story:

Three Ogres Visit Simone de Beauvoir

I was not really surprised that I was in Omaha, Nebraska, on a bright Saturday morning. I winced at my deficiency to understand how and when I had gotten there and proceeded to find the next bar.

Along the street no signs of imagery could be found. I crossed the plains to get a better view of where I was. I had no fear of Omaha, Nebraska, but I couldn't help feeling that I was somewhere else, even though I'd never been in Omaha before.

I got into town and noticed a considerably large hotel bar of French design. Upon entering, I saw a faceless man sitting on the floor playing jacks by himself. Above his head I noticed a sign that read:

Existentialism Is Dead

And so I went up the twenty-five steps of the staircase, because I didn't want to be in a room with a faceless man, sitting on the floor. Outside of the hotel-bar, no vultures circled, no cripples lingered.

I was really curious about the door, for, of course, I knew it would be cracked. But I swear I did not know who would be in the room, being the clues given were few.

I pushed open the door and found the last person on earth whom I would expect to find in Omaha, Nebraska: the legendary Simone de Beauvoir.

She looked up at me from under the flabby arm of a ten-foot, scale-encrusted ogre. Simone was casual in her glance — she looked as if she might have recognized me from somewhere.

Beauvoir proceeded to kiss the belly of the ogre. It made

me cry when the ogre said over and over, "I'm dying Beaver, I'm dying Beaver, and there is nothing we can do about it."

Right about that time, two ogres walked in who seemed to be brothers to the one holding Simone de Beauvoir. They broke in and nearly trampled me to death, but luckily they trampled over each other and fell away from them. They laughed and laughed and laughed and got off the floor.

The three ogres put Simone de Beauvoir at their center. I was still lying on the floor sweating. The two cheerful ogres grew somber when de Beauvoir started to cry. The ogres and Simone de Beauvoir began to hug and slobber over each other. The uninteresting dialog went like this:

– What has happened to us?

– We are growing extinct.

– Oh, Beaver; please take away the pain by fucking us gently.

– Didn't we care enough?

– (Simone) Oh, my pretty babies, my pretty babies, all is lost.

Simone de Beauvoir and the three scaly ogres of ten feet in length proceeded to fuck. They fucked with a fuck that was more than fuck. I wanted to fuck Beauvoir too, and come in her mouth, but then Sartre came into the room, and I fled down the staircase, passed the faceless man, hurried through the town, and found myself exhausted on the street with no imagery.

Marcel Hoon
Jackson, Mississippi
November 2005

After reading the thing, Victor said, "If I were you, I would go to John the Abecedarian and ask for an ablution because of this addled fragment of a work, and see if you can't find the Adlerian source of your afflatus." Marcel, even though he didn't like Victor, knew that Victor knew agraphia when he saw it. So, Marcel grew latescent as Alpha Centauri, and, with a renewed vigor of ague, went to his room.

The Absolute End

nature of theft:

The three ogres in the Simone de Beauvoir section of "Story" I obviously lifted from the major figures of 20th-century Existential philosophy. The three ogres represent, at least to my mind, Albert Camus, Martin Heidegger, and Jean-Paul Sartre, even though Sartre makes an appearance at the tail end of the story (he is still, apparently, one of the ogres as well). The ogres are cartoonish, in which I seem to be suggesting that the great spirit of Existentialism, the great austerity of that movement, was as doomed to extinction as Dada and Surrealism (Dada precedes Surrealism which precedes Existentialism). This too is ultimately the fate of the main character Marcel Hoon, whose name is stolen from Wallace Stevens' Mr. Hoon, for, after all, "Story" is a little tale that is about the impossibilities of writing anything meaningful at this point in literary history, at least from the point of view of the main narrator of the story, Louis E. Bourgeois. But enough, the story will speak, or not speak, for itself.

red wagon

nicole reid

In the shotgun house rented by the half-year, they haven't any time. The mother's typing mailing labels for a Lane Bryant catalog, paid a nickel apiece. But she's not permitted Wite-Out and is using her husband's old Underwood No. 5, pre-corrective tape era. She is twenty-seven weeks pregnant, and her belly sits her so far back, angling her wrists in such a way, that her 'H's are 'N's nine times out of ten. Her son chatters all day then kicks his ball against the typewriter stand, sending her fingers jumping. Invalid labels cost her four cents each.

She can hear the mockingbird perched high on a neighbor's chimney, twirtling and tweeting its many tongues. But what she listens to is the refrigerator's droning and clicking that seems louder than yesterday, about which she's supposed to decide if a repairman is necessary: her son's orange Push-Ups don't push up anymore, but ooze past the paper tube instead. How many labels would she have to type to pay for the repair? How many newspapers will her husband need to toss? How many labels buy a Push-Up?

Three.

She is trying to ignore her son playing with his G.I. Joe and Pooh doll on the rug behind her. She's got him in the bedroom so she can watch him and make — or lose — money at the same time. Her hands are only ever half at the keys; otherwise they're at her lips, her index finger raised to hush him.

Her son tugs at his shoelaces, wraps them round a leg of the bed, stumbles, then he starts to walk. The slap of his hands to the pine boards, the scuff of a knee to the tattered rug. He's waiting for her voice to come, because it has to. Because he is a bored boy, the first of five children who seems to know he is not, and never will be, alone. And so all these years he's just waiting.

She shifts in the chair, starts a label over. But she bites her lips and tongue, feels the inner halves of her first molars digging permanent dents.

He grabs up his dolls again, and begins narrating: "Pooh says, 'Shhhhhhhhh, Joe be quiet. Be good and follow me, Joe.'"

She types 'Smuth' for 'Smith', wonders in a split second — as she always does — if anyone will notice, if Janice Smith wouldn't prefer a more exotic name, then peels the label from the waxy sheet dotted here and there with empty space, and sticks the mistake to her ledger pad. The fridge will wait another month.

"Pooh's marching, march, march, march." Her son's knees and the bear's steps rumble across the slat floor, closer, closer. "Joe swings on a tree like a jungle," he says, and sends G.I. Joe flying right into her Achilles' tendon.

"Okay. Enough." She leaves off at Jamie Smith. "Nap time."

"No!" he cries, clutching his two dolls to him, then prancing them around back on the rug three feet behind where she sits at the cart, showing how silently he can be good.

But she gets up, and he's used to her like this, so he walks himself to his room, stands in front of his crib and lets her lift his almost three-year-old body over the gate. He's limp in her arms, limp and grey in the face. One doll rests tucked under each arm, gripped but not held near enough for any comfort. His body seems detached from his little head that tips back to see the ceiling, where she and his father hung a paper Calder mobile years ago. They snipped out each shape from a museum poster, then strung each on thread, and arranged them according to the original, from the ceiling: low enough to delight and high enough to outwit reaching arms. She'd been just as pregnant then as she is now, and without the crib put together yet, wife and husband lay side-by-side beneath their mobile, watching the way their breaths, so far below, could spin and twist the thread. She remembers his hand then, his hand that held hers and then went to her swollen stomach, the belly he told her again and again he found so erotic. He kissed it then, kissed her and pulled her to him, and they made love on their sides, beneath the sway of reds and blues and yellows, all turning with their breath. That was the last year of balance.

Now, instead of returning to her labels, she hovers

over the crib, left palm to her belly fearing movement, wanting to explain everything to her son. She looks into his blue eyes; eyes not light as the ocean, not dark as night; but something in-between, like where water and stars collide. But her son sees what must look like fright in her, and closes his eyes. What she would like to say is that the labels are for him. She wants him to understand what his quiet can buy: a big-boy bed for him when the baby comes, a truly frozen Push-Up, long days without the clackity typing, and naps born of her steady voice reading *Ferdinand the Bull.*

She hates that she puts him down to sleep like this, in a fight of wills, in a fight against his voice for which she would give back all the labels — each and every one she's ruined listening to his cooing warble almost indistinguishable from the mockingbird's — just to hear, to kneel with him on the rug, let him ask her the questions he must be asking himself, to hold him through his sleep. She vows to wake him soon.

Today is a Monday, the day that begins another week of league schedules and P.E. classes: the absurd string of oddly-houred jobs — all within walking distance so he won't need the car — that her husband has picked up to support his family and writing. Monday is the one good day because he is only gone from the house for his two paper routes and then out late for the adult ed volleyball class he coaches at the county rec center. (Tuesdays through Sundays, she hardly sees him at all.) But he is gone right now, walked out after bringing in the mail from the corner box. They'd both forgotten the car insurance in this week's budget — their budgets weekly since most of his jobs pay that way — but there it was: second notice.

"Didn't you pay this?" her husband said coming in, tugging open the envelope.

She looked up from lunch dishes she was clearing from the table. "What?" She'd seen the envelope before; the first notice. Fear washed through her, a reckless electricity. The first one disappeared weeks ago, and she hadn't remembered to look for it, hadn't remembered at all. "It wasn't written down anywhere; I lost it somewhere, I don't know," she said. "I guess I thought you'd paid it." She didn't know why she'd said that. It wasn't what she thought.

"Why would I have paid it? You write the checks, handle the budget. You run the show."

What was beneath the beard burned hot, red at the edges, red showing through. But she'd always wanted to laugh at such moments: a man with hands like this, giraffe-neck fingers, the arc of their curving to push up his glasses, to grip the bill, to find her cheek and hold it. That, the last was what his fingers were made for. Anything else was like alligator claws on a pianist.

"You're welcome to it anytime," she said.

He took a deep breath and spun the envelope on the table. "Will it wait?" He studied the fine print on the statement.

"Of course not." They really didn't need a car. He walked everywhere, so could she, or take a bus or something, even with their boy and another if she still had to then — she'd seen women with two and three young children waiting at bus stops; it could be done. But when had their life together — a life he'd fought her mother to let her embark on with a wretched

Catholic — become a process of eliminating every last convenience?

She refused to give up so easily, and so stepped willingly into irrationality. "I'm not driving around with a two year old and a baby, with no insurance," she shouted, letting their empty milk glasses crash to the bottom of the sink. "If you think I am, you're crazy!"

"You think I'd let you?" he said. "There's no way. I just thought they might go to a third notice." He held the paper again and was quiet.

Fighting like this, she had to struggle to stand. Spite, hatred, these were things impossible in him, those silly, tender cheeks and thin lips, hair the color of pennies. Nothing about him was convincing; he only looked scared.

She meant to kiss him, but only reached for the bill instead. "Well. I can't pay it." She stuffed the statement back into its envelope. "Can you?"

He shook his head. "What do we do?"

"Let's sell the rings." It's just what came out. She was willing, and she said it. They weren't what bound them. They were simple gold bands; hocked, they wouldn't even fix the refrigerator. But the look across his face; such a wound she'd never given him.

That's when he left, stormed out, the screen door slapping its frame seven times at least.

Now she sets tiny goals for herself. If she can finish a whole page of labels without errors, then she can go and get her son, wake him and pretend she knows where his father went. She isn't worried that he's quit her for good, that he's gone somewhere drinking at four in the afternoon, that he's run off with someone. He will be back, she has no doubt. But what does worry her, what eats at her fingertips when they hit the keys, is that she may have permanently damaged him. This is what she could not stand. She'd rather leave them both than know she's broken her husband or son.

And soon there will be three.

When she mistypes, she lessens her goal: the whole page of labels with only this one mistake. When she mistypes again, she allows the error, leaves it on the waxy paper, cheats. And after she does this once, she's unable to stop doing it. There is a small typo in each label in the last column because she cannot bear the quiet of the house.

She types faster, less accurately, and now leaves labels half-finished, half-smeared with over-typing of proper spellings and house numbers. With the last, she goes to her boy, sweeps shaggy bangs away from his eyes, removes one copper eyelash lost to the cheek.

She lifts her sleeping son from the crib, holds him at her side but cannot cradle his legs too because of her belly. She pushes him higher up her body, so that he bends over her shoulder, but can hardly support him like this so she lowers him to the floor, struggles to lay him there smoothly so he doesn't wake, then gets herself down without stumbling — rather like a camel, she thinks. She lies beside her son who will not wake now, her son who seems to want nothing more than sleep. She suspects he wants that because he thinks she will not be there with him. But she is. She is with him under his mobile, and their breath sends it turning, turning. She lies on her side, traces the shapes of her husband beside her, claiming those bits for him: her husband's thin lips, her husband's long fingers with their V-shaped cuticles, her own oceanic eyes — but never mind — and her husband's voice, if only he would wake.

She carries him downstairs like a sack of potatoes, even sings a song to rouse him, though he sleeps on. With a small blanket laid beneath, she fashions him into his Radio Flyer wagon — bought for two dollars at the block party yard sale even before she was pregnant the first time. She'd just wanted it, thought she would need it, felt an urgency about the thing. She pulls the wagon out the front door, easy over the step — not letting the screen door hit at all — then on and off the step stones to the sidewalk.

There is nothing but sun this afternoon, not even one cloud in the sky. The mockingbird twirtles and calls. Dogs bark blocks away, their owners or neighbors shouting at them to stop. The high school's late buses push and pull at their brakes, sending whooshes of far off life to her. She pulls the wagon — her son, she thinks, still willfully asleep — half a block to a playground abandoned for the pool on such a hot day. But there is the shade of a tulip poplar over a bench, and she parks the wagon there. She hums something made up and her son flashes open his eyes, then shuts them again, then opens and shuts trying to make sense of the white sky over this bed. She riffles his hair, her husband's especially red hair in this brightness, and goes on humming.

He makes his lips into an 'M', and almost says the

word for her, but then holds out his arms and she picks him up onto the very edge of her knees — all the lap she has left — feels his sneakers just above her ankles, and holds her breath for them to knock against her there, always.

"This is a funny bedroom you have, isn't it?" she says, pointing to the slide and swings. Still groggy, he only nods with his head cocked shyly, then arches his back over her belly, his forehead tucked beneath her chin. "I think your rug needs to be mowed." She kicks off her sandal and runs her toes through the leggy grass at her feet. He shows two teeth.

Soon he is up and trotting from bench to clover flower to bench and back out to white lace butterflies flitting away from him and back to bench. Each time, his trip is farther, but each time he comes back to her to explain what he's seen.

He runs to the swing-set and calls for her to come push. She perches his bottom in the rubber swing, reminds him to grip the chains, then sends him higher and higher, until they are both dizzy from staring up into the sun. Then she lets him ease back down, lower with each uncoordinated pump of his legs — something else she can claim for his father.

Her husband comes upon them here, struck dumb by the vision of late afternoon sunlight falling across her red dress — her belly entirely known to him, something he has claimed of hers — the hair she is always tugging back up into a bun or barrette, the hair he loves to feel against his cheek when they kiss, cascading freely at her temples and down her back. Their boy so marvelously happy. Their voices mingle and become one: each of them rising, dipping to find the other's pitch; the way one rounds an 'O' so fully and then both do. And she smiles, as if she already knows she will hear this story each time he slides into bed behind her. When he's given up on a scene or chapter at the end of the day because all he can think of is her red dress.

He goes to them. There is no stiffening, just the rush of their boy to him, him sweeping his boy up into his arms, into the air. And she walks to him, too, finding no fear in his face, just a moment of regret for the door slamming after him, for one Monday lost to a walk round and round the blocks of the neighborhood trying to make sense of money, instead of his knees beside their son's on the rug in the bedroom, whispering riddles and kisses while she tapped out labels for nickels.

He presses one silly hand to her cheek, the other to her belly waiting for a nudge of life to answer.

She shuts her eyes but takes his long fingers to her mouth, kisses his ring, and opens her eyes. "A sort of wish," she says.

"For what?"

"For this, just this."

nature of theft:

One night after a visiting writer's reading, my mentor Richard Bausch drove that writer, Andrea Barrett, another student, and me back to campus along a route that would pass by his old house. It was a tiny place right up on the road. Nothing lovely about it, really. But Dick told us about a time he and his then wife, very pregnant with their second child, saw each other after a big fight about how to pay the bills. She'd worn red and stood in the ragged and dusty playground next door waiting for him to come back, which of course he did. The sun on the red of her dress was the color of love, was something I wanted and had no idea how to make it mine. So I wrote about it.

king of kings (of leon)

craig bayne

Voice 1: …And he's thinking, *Christ, I'm here with my mum*. She doesn't even drink, so Adam is bored out of his mind and, to be honest, he doesn't even like the band. Who does, anyway? The Kings of Leon are crap — he only bought the ticket to see the support band — but he took his mum along because she actually likes the bunch of rednecks.

So he's hanging about, watching the crowd, watching anything except the band or his mum's dancing, and to kill time he nips to the bar, but, on the off chance, bumps into Dave who's got two spare passes to the afterparty — meet the band, free booze, lots of girls… take your mum? Pfff… Well, he did what I would have done: the crowd's leaving, the gig's over, he's standing there, blocking everyone's way with these two guest passes outstretched, mulling it over — he's only got a few pounds in his pocket, but screw it — he ditches his mum right there and then and heads to the party.

It's up in some little private room at the top of the building, so he climbs the stairs, flashes his pass to enormous security guards every two minutes, there's record execs and all sorts of leaching bastards all over the place, he climbs more stairs, still showing the pass, there's an empty private bar, he shows the pass again, up even more stairs, and, finally, he comes to the door. You know the Germans, they've got this word *schwelleangst*, means something like 'fear of the threshold', you know it?

Voice 2: How the hell would I know it?

Voice 1: Well, it's for like, you know when you're just about to walk into an art gallery, or a dentist's waiting room, and you get that feeling, that sort of… 'I don't belong here' anxiety?

Voice 2: Sure.

Voice 1: Well, that's *schwelleangst*, fear of the threshold. So Adam opens the door and —

Voice 2: What the hell are you going on about that for?

Voice 1: What?

Voice 2: German.

Voice 1: What?

Voice 2: This bloody spiel on German.

Voice 1: Shut it, I'm telling you the story. So he opens the door and the place is crammed with your usual long-haired indie-schmoozers, drinking cans of Red Stripe and stroking their indie-beards, dropping the names of hundreds of bands 'they know quite well' to seventeen-year-old girls, who, never having heard of half of the bands, are busy thinking how this old guy's indie-beard sort of makes him look like her dad.

Anyway, cutting a long story short, he ends up ploughing the free booze and chatting up this young girl, who's drunk as a priest and covered in bright red lipstick. He's doing his best, you know, name dropping bands is the mating ritual here, so he's visualising his iPod playlist, but the girl, suddenly without warning, just walks off. Jarred, from the Kings of Leon, has just walked into the room and she's off like a shot, with the rest of the young girls, to cream herself in front of him, and Adam, ever trying, chases her over, still thinking he's in with a chance.

Voice 2: He's a bloody idiot. Here, d'you want another drink?

Voice 1: Yeah, but wait a minute, I'll finish the story.

Voice 2: But I kind of need to go to the toilet.

Voice 1: Well, you can just wait a bloody minute. So, Jarred's standing there, right, one hand in his pocket, one hand with a cigarette, faded blue jeans, a kind of hairy hick James Dean vibe going on and he's surrounded by this ring of teenage girls, three deep.

Voice 2: Bastard.

Voice 1: Yeah, I know. So he's standing there asking these girls what they thought of the gig. It's all 'Amazing!' and 'The best I've *ever* seen!' and Adam walks up, still trying to impress this girl, and smart-arse that he is, tells the guy what *he* thought of it — that it was total shit.

Voice 2: Really?

Voice 1: Yeah, he said it was absolute bollocks, that the sound was terrible — gave him a hundred reasons why he didn't like it. Well, after a stunned silence, turns out that the guy appreciated his honesty, actually quite liked him, and they hung about for a bit then Jarred invites him to come back to the hotel for a party.

So Adam gets to the hotel and walks into the reception. The place is rammed to the walls with hammered teenagers and pissed record-label suits. He's giving it all his best chat, know what I mean, he's that sort of guy, schmoosing people 'in the business' and looking cool in front of the girls. He's always been like that really, a bit of a try-hard, you know?

Voice 2: Yeah, he's an arsehole, there's no disputing it.

Voice 1: Well, he ends up getting with that girl, the one with the lipstick. Buys her a few drinks, and he told me that — whether it's true or not, you know what he's like—he ends up fingering her in the toilet.

Voice 2: Bullshit.

Voice 1: Take it or leave it, but either way, about an hour later he's sitting with her at the hotel bar, record execs in skinny jeans crawling all over the girls like bearded maggots, and Adam's girl — absolutely wrecked by the way — reaches for her drink and falls right off her stool headfirst.

So, embarrassed I imagine, he helps her up from the floor—but he gets a look at her when he's picking her up, and she's totally hammered. Not that 'making-an-arse-of-yourself-on-the-dancefloor' hammered, she's more 'eyes-pointing-the-wrong-way, oh-shit-she's-about-seventeen-years-old-and-about-to-pass-out' hammered. And he's freaking out a bit, feeling sort of responsible as he bought her all that booze.

He sits her on a couch and gets her a glass of water, but she passes out anyway and he's stuck with her — nobody knows her, nobody gives a fuck about her — everyone's either swanning around being too important, or, are far too busy trying hard to look important and couldn't be bothered to help her. Then he's worried, not for the girl, but for himself — this makes him look bad. He's wanting to get rid of her, and quickly. So he asks this beast, this brick-shit-house guy with a utility belt, a roadie or a technician or something, if he's got a room in the hotel. The guy gives him his spare key and tells Adam to go up and put her in the bed, as apparently the roadie's leaving in a few minutes anyway.

Well, I think he pretty much had to drag her into the elevator, her shoes scuffing black marks along the hotel floor and everything. Imagine him: flashing awkward smiles to the Kings of Leon and the pensioner couples wishing they'd booked another hotel that night. He hauls her down the corridor, shuffles her into the room and drops her limp body onto the bed — then it's lights off, problem solved, and back down the stairs for another drink.

So he hangs about for another hour and a bit, just mooching the free booze and watching the dregs of the party fondle each other. Apparently the Kings of Leon are dicks, cokeheads and up their own arse and that. They only talk about themselves and never pass their joints. He did say that he got talking to one of the guys in the support band who was alright — into philosophy or something, you know Adam's into all that rubbish.

Voice 2: Yeah, he talks some amount of crap. Here, listen, I'm going to go to the toilet…

Voice 1: Can you not just wait a bloody minute?

…So, yeah, an hour goes past, and he decides to go up and check on the girl, but he gets to the room, opens the door, and the roadie guy's in there, trousers off, holding the girl — who's still completely passed out by the way, got her propped up — trying to get her bra off.

The girl's unconscious, you know, so drunk that you could swing her about and she'd never wake up. Adam's thinking *fuck, what do I do*, so he goes into the room and shuts the door behind him. The roadie roars at him to fuck off, but fair play to him, he holds his ground and just stands there.

The roadie gets up. Moves over and sits on the other single bed in the room, and just stares at him. Adam's thinking this guy is twice his size — and let's face it, Adam's five–foot-six and pretty effeminate. If it comes to a fight, he doesn't stand a chance. And I don't know why he didn't just leave to go get someone, but he goes and stands between the two single beds, like a barrier between the roadie and the girl, and just stares right back at him.

He's standing up, looking down at the guy and thinking that the height gives him a bit of a psychological advantage — but the roadie, still in his pants, grabs him by the arm and pushes him down on to the bed. Just to show him, you know, remind him who's going to kick the fuck out of who.

So they're both sitting there on opposite beds, staring at each other, just a small table between them, and Adam realises there's no way of avoiding it, this is coming to a fight. *This is coming to a fight*, he thinks, *and I'm going to have to hit him first, and hard enough that he doesn't get back up and hit me*. There's a lamp on the table and it's got a fat wooden bottom on it — he lunges for it, to smash the guy in the skull with it, but it doesn't move. It's screwed to the table.

Voice 2: Fuck.

Voice 1: Yeah, the guy looks at him. Looks at the lamp, and calmly, too calmly, asks, *what are you doing*?

And I don't know what he did, fiddled with the switch or something, said he was just playing with it. Fuck knows, but he just sat there, waiting for the roadie to punch him. And the roadie's just sitting there looking back at him, watching him.

Then Adam, just to kill the tension, picks up a book from the table. It's a Gideon Bible, like in every room at the hotel, and he thumbs through the pages, face down in it, still waiting to get his head caved in, accepting his fate. And like I was saying, you know how he's into reading and philosophy or whatever?

Voice 2: Yeah.

Voice 1: Well, he asks the guy if he's ever read Revelations. It's the last book in the Bible — don't look at me like that, I went to a Catholic high school — but yeah, obviously, the guy has no idea what he's talking about, and the question, more than anything else, has just sent him completely off track.

So Adam starts preaching to the roadie about Revelations, not that he's mad about Jesus or that, but, you know how he's always going on about some bollocks, cornering some poor bastard at a party and talking the ears off him.

Anyway, he starts ranting about this bit in Revelations, tells the guy what it's all about — he's going on and on about the end of the world and the final battle between good and evil: Satan rises from the sulphurous pits of hell and takes control of the people. The beast opens the seven seals and the earth is torn apart by massive earthquakes. All the people of the world, except for the virtuous Christians, become slaves of the beast.

Everyone has a choice, to fight with the beast or to fight on the side of God. The final battle takes place, the beast and Satan are defeated and all of their followers, all of the people who chose to fight against God, are cast down to the sulphurous pits to burn for eternity. This fire isn't like the fire here on earth: this fire isn't made for cooking or heating, it gives off no light and it burns the flesh without destroying it. The tormented souls are scorched for eternity without the release of death, and then, in complete darkness, the torn earth will join back together and entomb them inside itself forever.

Voice 2: But what happened with Adam?

Voice 1: Well, he freaked the guy out, didn't he? Apparently the guy just got up, pulled on his trousers, didn't say a thing to him, and just left. Adam reckons he must have had one of those brutally religious upbringings — that he just snapped or something.

Voice 2: Fucking hell, so he was stuck in the room with the half-naked girl?

Voice 1: Yeah, he went to sleep and she was sick on herself.

nature of theft:

This story was overheard in a bar in Glasgow. The two guys, fortunately, had no concept of acceptable volume. As I sat with my girlfriend, actually holding the flyer for this stolen stories publication, I started to make notes on the back of it.

what is it that you want?

alison key

"Ron?"

He murmurs something in his sleep.

"Are you awake, Ron?"

"Go to sleep, Jackie."

His voice is thick, as if his tongue is swollen or he has a mouth full of water.

I plump up the pillows and prop them behind me.

He sleeps like a baby, my Ron. His head isn't cluttered with dreams.

Me, I've always dreamed of winning the lottery.

Ron says it's a waste of time and good money, but I still buy a ticket every week for the Saturday draw. I've always thought that if I ever won I'd like to see a bit more of the world. Some of the places on the *Discovery Channel* look really brilliant. But Ron's not like me.

"The heat brings me out in a rash," he said.

"You don't know that because you've never been anywhere really hot," I said. "Besides, we went to Malta that time and you were fine. I don't remember having to rub calamine lotion on your back in Malta."

The truth is, he's not interested.

I read in a magazine that when you win the jackpot, they send someone round. The winners don't just get a letter or a phone call, someone comes to see them in person. As I was reading, I had this picture in my head of a man wearing a raincoat. A beige one from Marks and Spencer, double-breasted, a belt with a large buckle and button-down flaps over the shoulders. A man with a Hollywood kind of smile. And a cheque in a leather briefcase, which he would only open after he'd checked the person's identity and inspected the winning ticket. I imagined a cameraman too, waiting outside until all the paperwork was done. Not everyone would want their picture taken. Suppose their hair was a mess, or they'd just got up and hadn't had time to get dressed. And some people would want to stay anonymous because of all the dreadful begging letters, and who could blame them?

The magazine article had stories of jackpot winners. One man went back to his old job. He said he'd got bored and his wife had had enough of him being under her feet all day. I thought to myself, that'll be my Ron. If he won the lottery, he'd be back in the shop the next day, frying fish.

There are times when the only thing Ron ever seems interested in is fish.

Back when we were courting, we'd be at the pictures or walking in the park and I suspected then he'd rather have been fishing. Not that he didn't love me. He just loved fish.

I used to go with him to the canal. No way was I ever going to eat anything pulled out of that filth, but Ron didn't care. He'd sit under his big umbrella, even when it wasn't raining, his line dribbling across the greasy film of stagnant water. I thought it would be nice for us to talk, to make plans, but he liked to sit there in silence, staring into space.

"There's carp and roach in that there canal," he said. "I can't catch roach and talk."

I read *Great Expectations* that summer. Sitting on a wooden stool by the canal next to Ron. I reckoned I needed a big book to see me through if it was going to work out between us and *Great Expectations* was the thickest I found. That Marjorie Wallace had a nerve, raising her eyebrow and sucking the air through her teeth when she stamped my card. I knew what she was thinking alright. She was thinking, I bet she'll never finish this. Cheeky cow. Well I did. I read the whole book on that towpath. It took a few renewals, but I finished it. Ron moved the Tupperware box of maggots away from me and we crouched under the umbrella like a couple of bookends, Ron fishing, and me reading *Great Expectations*.

I glance over at Ron before turning off the light and wonder where the time has gone.

On the bedside table is the digital radio he bought me last Christmas.

"Use the earphones," he said, "so I can get a decent night's sleep."

Years ago when I couldn't sleep, I'd sit in bed smoking cigarettes and reading magazines like some old film star, exhaling thick blue smoke through my nostrils into the night. Now, I listen to the World Service.

I never thought I'd be the sort of person to listen to the World Service. At first, I didn't know where half the places were. It's midnight in Lima or Lagos or Lahore the announcer would say and I'd have to go to the library and look it up. It's a real education. I learned about crop rotation in Guyana and why the Chinese love English TV.

Once there was a programme about a man in India who ate a car.

"What do you mean, he ate a bloody car?" Ron said.

"He ate a car," I said. "The whole thing. Tyres, seats, engine, everything."

"Don't be daft."

"It's true," I said. "It was on the World Service. It took him nearly six years. It was in India."

"Well, there you go then," he said, rolling his eyes and disappearing behind the sports pages.

I ignored him and thought for a moment.

"It just shows you," I said. "Anything is possible."

I wait for my eyes to get used to the gloom. Ron's steady breathing soon drops away into silence. That's when I know he's well and truly gone. I wait for it to start up again. Soft long breaths, a faint, funny little whistle down one nostril. I try breathing at the same time as him, hoping some of his sleep will rub off on me.

When Ron came home with the idea that we should buy the fish and chip shop on the corner of Canal Road, I was in the middle of sliding the iron round a shirt button. My hand stopped for a moment too long and I almost singed the cotton. The children were still small then and I was dead against it.

"You'll come home every night smelling of old chip fat," I said.

Ron fishing every Sunday was bad enough. He came home filthy. I made him strip everything off in the hallway and get straight in the bath, while I put his clothes in the machine.

"Besides," I said, "there's a reason that shop's been closed for so long."

Ron said that people had their reasons. He said the shop was in a good spot and we should give it a go, but even when he was putting on his old wedding suit to go for the bank loan, I still wasn't sure. It seemed like a lot of hard work to me. Besides, once the children were all at school I planned to go back to my typing. But he came home with beer on his breath.

"It's a deal," he said.

He was up all night, excited as a child on Christmas Eve. For once, I was asleep before him.

The shop was in a state. There were so many bills and old newspapers on the floor, Ron had to shove the door with his shoulder to get it open. Dead flies lay scattered on the window ledge like wizened currants. There were a couple of pot-bound geraniums with crisped leaves. A broken venetian blind hung at an angle, its slats splayed and twisted. We inspected the fryers. They hadn't been used for ages and the fat had turned rancid. When Ron opened the freezer door, the stench was unbearable. On one wall there was a calendar with a picture of a Chinese palace and all the months printed below it in red ink. On the other was a plastic clock whose hands had stopped at exactly 7.30. And behind the counter, mounted on the back wall, was a large glass box.

"What the hell is that?" I said.

"It's a fish," Ron said.

"I'm not having a stuffed fish in here," I said. "It's unhygienic."

Ron went to have a closer look.

"Come and have a look at him, Jackie," he said. "He's a beauty."

I wiped my forefinger across the front of the glass, leaving a wavering trail through the grease and dust, took off my glasses and peered inside. I'd never seen a fish that big before. It was huge, at least two foot, with bronze scales like it had been sprayed in metallic paint and yellow fins. Its miserable mouth was open, exposing hundreds of tiny sharp teeth like a saw, gawping at me, gawping at it.

"It's staring at me," I said. "It gives me the creeps."

"He's tropical," Ron said, smiling. "Maybe a jack or a trevally or something."

"It's disgusting."

Ron laughed and gave my waist a squeeze.

"Jackie, my love," he said, kissing me on the cheek. "You're looking at a very rare Chinese good luck fish, probably close to extinction in the wild. He'll bring us good luck, he will."

I laughed too then and kissed him back.

"You and your fish."

My fingernails were never the same after all the cleaning we did. They didn't stop breaking. I had to scrub everything. And I could've filled the old mill dam again, the amount of water I went through. It turned brown in seconds, so I couldn't just wash everything once. And I polished the tiles and the stainless steel fryers until I could see in them to put on my lipstick. Ron gave the walls a fresh coat of eggshell. He unscrewed the old fish off the wall, cleaned the glass and put it back up again. We bought new dripping for the fryers. Ron bought a new potato peeler and chipper. I got us white coats to wear.

"It's a chippy Jackie, not a bloody fishmongers," Ron said.

"They make us look professional," I said. "Besides, I'm not having batter getting over everything."

At first, the smell got to me, it soaked right into the pores of my skin. I had to wash my hair every night. But Ron installed a shower in the back, so now we come home spotless and smelling of shower gel.

Ron does all the frying and I serve. The heat from the fryers steams up my glasses and besides, people like to chat while they're waiting and I'm better at talking to people than Ron. I'm also better at adding up. Not that it's rocket science. We've stuck to traditional haddock and chips, plus peas and fish cakes. None of your pies or sausages or curry sauces, although we do have a large jar of pickled eggs on the counter because Ron insisted, but they've been there as long as I can remember. No one round here will eat them.

I admit, there are some days when I long to have a job where I'm not on my feet all day. I catch myself thinking it would be nice to be back in an office with the girls, somewhere cool, with proper air conditioning, carpets and lifts. Somewhere smelling of air freshener, furniture polish and clean white paper. But there are not many days when I think like this. I've grown to love the shop almost as much as Ron does.

Today, being a Wednesday, we were closed. Ron was at the wholesalers and I'd only popped in to run some potatoes through the peeler, ready for tomorrow's lunchtime rush. The peeling machine makes a right old racket, and what with all those potatoes thumping around inside, it was a wonder I even heard the banging on the door.

I thought it was kids messing about at first, but when I went out into the shop I could see it was a man in a raincoat. He had his face up to the door, peering through the glass into the shop. A mobile phone was glued to one ear. When he saw me, he waved.

"We're closed," I shouted.

"Can I have a word?" he mouthed.

"We're closed," I shouted.

He looked vaguely familiar. He was very young. His face was all pink and scrubbed, his coat belt was trailing on the ground. He stamped his feet on the pavement, shifting his weight from one foot to the other. It was a bitterly cold day. I must have felt a bit sorry for him because I lifted the serving counter, went round to the front and undid the bolts on the door. I had to stretch up to undo the top one. He was standing inches away from me, with just the thin glass between us and I suddenly felt shy and held onto my T-shirt. I didn't want it riding up, showing him a slice of my belly, not at my age and after four kids. I bent down, slid the bottom bolt back and opened the door. A blast of icy air hit my face.

"How can I help you?" I said.

The man in the raincoat held out his hand and gave

me a card.

"I'm Jake Preston from the *Evening Post*. I wonder if I could have another look at your fish."

He nodded towards the glass case on the back wall.

I remembered him from yesterday. Fish and chips twice, wrapped. I was sprinkling on the salt, waiting for him to tell me when to stop, but he was gazing over my shoulder in a bit of a dream.

"I've not been able to get it off my mind."

"My fish?"

"Can I have a closer look?"

I nodded and moved aside to let him pass.

"People said there was one in a chippy round here, but I never believed them," he said, rubbing the palms of his hands together. "I thought it was just a rumour, you know, an urban myth. My editor is going to love this."

"Look, love — "

"They say his brother once worked in a chip shop. Is that right? Is that how come you have it? Did he give it to you himself?"

"It was here when we bought the shop," I said.

The man in the raincoat studied me.

"My God," he said. "You don't know what you've got on your hands, do you?"

I was beginning to regret letting him in.

"No," I said.

"Well, I may be wrong, but if this fish is what I think it is, it'll change your life. It's a Damien Hirst."

I was confused.

"I don't know about that. Look love, I think you need to speak to my husband. He's the one who knows about fish."

He pulled a notebook and biro from his pocket.

"I can see the headlines now," he said, sweeping his hand in an arc in front of him. "*What a Catch!*"

He laughed.

I laughed too, even though I still had no idea what he was on about. I glanced at the card he'd given me.

"Shall I phone my husband?"

"Just a couple more questions, then I'll get straight back to the office and make a few calls. What about *Today's Headlines, Tomorrow's Fish and Chip Paper*? No, maybe not."

"We don't use newspaper any more," I said.

"Ah yes, of course. EC regulations."

I watched him write some squiggles in his notebook.

"Is that shorthand?" I asked.

But he had his back to me again. I stared at his hair, blond and straight, cut in steps down his head.

"He's an ugly bastard isn't he, if you'll excuse my language? Not my idea of art. Still. I hope you've got it insured. Could be worth thousands. Will you sell it? What will you do with the money? Of course, as I said, don't start quoting me just yet, we'll have to check with the experts, an auction house maybe, or even the man himself. Let me take down a few details now, it won't take long, and I'll be back as soon as I can with a photographer for some shots. What did you say your name was?"

I felt lightheaded. The shop started to spin. I couldn't hear the man's voice any more. All I could hear were the potatoes rattling in the peeler, thundering in my ears. There'd be nothing left of them. I put my hand on the cool, steel counter to steady myself.

"Would you like a cup of tea?" I asked.

So we both went round the back, and I turned the peeler off and put the kettle on. The man in the raincoat explained that the fish wasn't really a fish. Well, it was a real fish, but it might also be a work of art that only people like Elton John and Madonna could afford. The artist was world famous. He told me a lot of things, and all the time he was talking I was just sitting there, my mouth opening and closing so much I must have looked like a great, big, bloody fish myself. There were no sounds coming out of me, and I just kept thinking about how much a piece of haddock cost and wondering why anyone in their right mind would want to spend so much money on a fish.

After the man left, I went to the library and typed the name he gave me into Google. There were lots more fish in glass boxes and a shark in a big tank. There was even a cow, a lovely black and white Friesian, cut in half. It made no sense. I wondered what Ron would make of it all. He wouldn't believe it.

I always thought I'd love to win the lottery and this is like winning the lottery, but my head aches trying to make sense of it all.

"Ron?"

The bed pitches and rolls as Ron shifts and turns over in his sleep, his back facing me. He takes up more of the bed than he used to. Ron's always been on the large side, but tonight his back looks huge, like something dredged from the bottom of the sea. His arm is wrapped round his shoulder, hugging himself. His fingers, relaxed and gentle, float down towards the big mole on his back.

"It's the shape of Africa," I told him once, tracing round its edges with the tips of my fingers.

There is a faint whistle.

His hair is all mussed. Ron always did have a good head of hair. I can still see the black in it. When we were first married he had hair like ink, all Brylcreamed and shining. I made him sleep with his head on a towel so that it wouldn't make a mess on the pillows. The back of his neck is furrowed like a ploughed field. I wonder when that happened.

"Are you asleep, Ron?"

Ron mumbles something.

"Ron?"

I nudge him ever so softly.

"Ron?"

He rolls on his back, his eyes still closed.

"What is it Jackie? I have to be up at six. Can't it wait?"

"I was thinking about the lottery."

"Is that it? You woke me up to tell me that?"

"I was thinking, suppose I told you you'd won the jackpot."

"Jackie, I don't even do the lottery, how the hell am I going to win the jackpot?"

"Just suppose, Ron. What would you do with the money? Do you think you'd travel? Would you like to go to Australia and go fishing on the Barrier Reef? It said on the World Service you can see the Barrier Reef from space. What do think, Ron?"

I switch on the light.

Ron mumbles something under his breath. He opens

his eyes and looks at me.

"Jackie. I don't want to go fishing on the Barrier Reef. I don't want to win the lottery. Right now, I just want to go to sleep."

"Are you saying you don't want to win the jackpot? It could change our lives, Ron."

Ron sighs.

"What's wrong with the lives we've got?"

"Nothing. But is there nothing you'd like to change?"

"Go to sleep."

"You could stop working. We could sell the shop and retire to the coast. Would you like that?"

"I thought you liked the shop?"

"I do."

"Jackie, I don't know why I'm even having this conversation."

"I was just thinking."

"Well, stop your thinking now please, turn off the bloody light and go to sleep."

He rolls back on his side, pulling the duvet with him. I lean over, switch off the bedside light and sit in the dark with Ron's fish still swimming round in my head. I can feel the buttons on the mattress pressing into the backs of my thighs.

At some point, I must doze off.

I dream I'm diving into a deep blue ocean, so deep there is no sound. It's full of brightly coloured fish. There are angelfish and butterflyfish with black and yellow stripes, and others striped in black and white like humbugs. There are parrotfish, blue and transparent as the ocean itself, and jacks with electric blue fins and tails. And flashes of orange clownfish and swathes of silver. And thousands and thousands of tiny champagne bubbles pour out of their mouths. And out of mine too. And at first they make me giggle and my head fizz and I start laughing. But then I start choking on all the bubbles. I cough and splutter. I can't breathe. The water is so full of fish I can't move. A large purple fish with a rubbery yellow mouth moves close to my face and I start to sink.

I wake with a start, hitting the back of my head against the wall.

I wait three days for him to come back to the shop. I spot him loitering outside as I'm wrapping a portion of chips and my heart misses a beat. My hand goes up to my head. My hair is a state. I strain my neck to see if he's brought his photographer with him, but he's alone.

When the shop clears, he comes in.

"Hello again," he says.

I glance over my shoulder. Ron is in the back, getting more fish out of the freezer.

"Let's go outside," I say, wringing my overall in my hands.

We stand on the pavement in the freezing cold.

"This is all rather embarrassing," he says, "so I'll come straight to the point. It appears I was wrong about your fish."

Ron is sleeping like a baby. I lift the duvet and swing my legs out of bed.

The whole house is bathed in a blue-grey light. I put the kettle on and sit at the kitchen table in the dark waiting for it to boil. The house creaks and groans.

The fridge in the corner hums, the motor purrs. The radiators burp and gurgle even though the central heating is not due to come on for another couple of hours.

My bare feet start to numb on the cold lino, but I sit like this, staring out of the kitchen window for a while, drinking tea.

I should have known he didn't really know what he was talking about. Reporters will tell you anything to get a story. And compared to my Ron, what did he know about fish? He wouldn't stop apologising about raising my hopes, but all the time he was saying sorry I just felt this enormous sense of relief.

"You don't really know what you want, Jackie," Ron once said. "You only think you do."

I prefer to think I've changed my mind. Maybe it would have been good to travel when I was younger, but not now. I know what Ron means about the heat. It makes my legs swell. And last summer, my fingers got so fat I thought I'd have to go to the jewellers and get Mr Simmons to cut off my wedding ring.

I make another cup of tea and look out of the window some more, trying to do what Ron would do. Stop thinking and just stare into space.

Then, just as my eyelids begin to grow heavy and I think I should go back to bed, a lovely thing happens.

It starts to snow.

My gasp fills the empty kitchen. I open the back door and stand there, hands cupped around my tea, watching the flakes of snow float gently down onto the lawn. The sky is thick. The whole world, silent. Sleeping. It is endless. I watch the snow floating, like scraps of torn doilies, softly to the ground and I feel completely calm. I have a sudden urge to run upstairs and wake Ron. I want him to see the snow too, but I'm transfixed. Besides, he probably wouldn't believe what a beautiful thing he was missing.

After awhile, I realise the ground is too wet and it's not going to settle. And then the flakes get smaller and smaller. They start to speed up and soon it's sleet. Soon the snow will be gone.

I go back to bed. Ron is lying on his belly, his face squashed into the pillow, his arm flung across the mattress. I squeeze myself into the space next to him. The sheet is ice-cold and I'm shivering. Ron lets out a soft sigh. I can feel the heat from his body and I try not to touch it with my frozen one. I lie there, listening to the rhythm of his breathing.

nature of theft:

I stole this story from a newspaper article. I read that the owner of my local childhood fish and chip shop had just sold a Damien Hirst fish, which had been mounted on the shop's wall for many years, for over £250,000. (Hirst's brother had worked in the shop as a student and Hirst had given the owner the fish as a gift early in his career.) I know the chip shop and I remember the fish, although I had no idea it was a Damien Hirst. My first thought was, wouldn't it be great. And then I thought, maybe not.

teehanu

nick holdstock

They had begun four hours ago, in the dark, in the womb of the dunes. The two of them had sat cross-legged, she visualising her ovum, he encouraging his sperm. After a while she opened her eyes and said, “David, I love you.” He told her he felt the same, and then they closed their eyes again, and then they were making love without touching at all. They did this for another hour, and only then did they start to kiss, because, as they had both agreed, Creation was a sacred process that should not be rushed.

When she said, “I love you,” for the sixty-eighth time, he began to push more slowly, to almost pull out of her, and she was now beyond orgasm, she was in some other place, a high plateau with sparking light where there was no need for breath and the chakras were open 24-7 like the Korean shop near the pier. Her eyes were closed, and they were open, and there were wise Tibetan yaks which saw the light that lived in her while David moved his sensitive penis in and out. It was a place without a name, because it had no need for one, but if it had, its name would be *Teehanu*. A land where women run with the wolves, where women are the wolves, and the pulse, when it arrived, was the true meaning of *sudden*. She heard, she felt things start to hum, the atoms dancing as they charged, as every grain of sand, every blade of grass, as every water-turn of wave was fully expectant. And as she told people later, "I didn't need to *tell* David. He knew, because I knew, and we were the same person, like brother and sister, y'know?"

David began thrusting harder, and Skye raised her tired legs higher, and then the sun rose out of the sea like a great and significant egg. It cracked its red light on them and they stared in each other's eyes — her blue eyes looked viridian, his green eyes seemed topaz — and with a simultaneous sigh, they came. Then the heralds called from her namesake; the waves pounded a victory song.

They lay together, him in her, and it felt like the natural state, the way things ought to be. A jogger passed, and paused, still running, the soles of his trainers printing the sand till he saw Skye's arm twitch. Then he moved off down the beach while David's sperm swam on. They struggled like tiny salmon, and, as on any great journey, friends were made, and friends were lost, and whenever David sees footage of tadpoles he recalls that story about the race where people keep walking or else they get shot, a story which is by Richard Bachman, who is actually Stephen King, and he read this and other stories in the summer before Skye and he met, when he was trying to buy weed but couldn't ever seem to score, and finally he just sat in the park with a load of books because maybe then, when he'd stopped looking, the weed would fucking come to *him*. And so he sat and read while trying to look like the kind of guy who wanted to buy drugs. Sometimes this group of rich girls came and sat in the park and did some kind of exercise that involved them bringing their feet up to their thighs while standing with their hands out and trying not to fall and then, after they'd done this for twenty minutes, a blonde girl with long, tanned legs and breasts like fists would clap her hands and they'd sit in a circle and hold hands and make noises that weren't proper words and the first few times he totally cracked up because it wasn't the *Sixties*.

And when Skye and David got dressed they didn't feel the same. It was like they'd never worn pants or shirts, as if their actions had restored them to some original condition, to a state before cities or cars when the only burdens people carried were firewood and water. They walked the long line of the beach, surf frothing at their heels, Life beginning inside her. When they got home they drank mineral water and fell quickly asleep.

When Skye woke it was dark again and she could not remember her dream. She lay next to David and wondered if those hours on the beach had ever happened at all. But there was sand in her hair, salt in her pores, that feeling of starting again. She knew she was still herself, but now, maybe more so. Now all the worries were gone. All the unworthy suspicion. They would walk their path together, first as two, then as three, but always, they would be one.

She got up and opened the window and the night

came in. The hiss and click of the sprinklers. The scent of Cereus, Queen of the Night, as she flowered and bloomed.

She swung one of her legs out the window and then straddled the sill. The wet lawns shone in the light and she saw no one except for Jesús on his nightly round. She wished there was no need for fences, barriers, locks or walls, for armed and highly trained personnel to perpetually circle their compound like Tibetan monks at prayer. She did not want these things. She wanted to be close to people. But there was the problem of Hate. The world was full of people who had never met their true selves, who never breathed from their diaphragms or thought about White Light. And this had nothing to do with money — some of the most enlightened people were also incredibly poor.

Skye stroked the skin of her foot and then a breeze did the same. The air was warm and with a new scent, something like marjoram, or sage, and she looked at David, who loved her so much, and then she turned and saw Jesús stop to light a cigarette. It pulsed and glowed in the dark and she thought, no, she *felt*, the satisfaction *he* must feel from making people safe. He was a guardian, a true protector, and when that one-eyed man who lived under the pier followed her home, scaled the fence, knocked on her door and burst in, screaming, Jesús was immediately there, and although violence was never good (and could only beget more violence), Jesús really had no choice. If he hadn't broken the man's arms, then his jaw, then his nose, the one-eyed man would have done the same to her.

After the paramedics left, she sat on her blood-spattered sofa and cried and Jesús put his arm round her and what they did together afterwards had nothing to do with cheating. They had shared a terrible thing, an awful thing, and if they did it in the shower, on the floor, it was only to restore the balance by sharing something of beauty.

Jesús walked out of sight. Skye got into bed. She spooned up to David, who turned and put his arm around her, and that was how she fell asleep, and that was how she woke next morning, with him, with Life inside her, with the walls painted in sun, with the chorus of birds outside, feeling utterly free of want, completely at peace with things, and this Moment stretched for nine months, because she was in it, she was *of* it, and although David did not believe in Moments, he held crystals above her stomach, ran hundreds of herbal baths, walked twenty blocks for goji berries when he was hungover. He held her hand while she chanted and breathed in a room with orange walls and sometimes there weren't enough mats so he had to sit on the floor which made his ass really numb. David got used to the look in her eyes, that dreamy, unfocused gaze, as if she was looking through a hole in a fence reserved only for Mothers. Sometimes he came home and found her saying "I love you" to her belly while shining a flashlight on it.

The baby pushed her belly out. They talked about a name. David said, "What about Lyle?"

"No," she said. "That's a boy's name."

"Maybe it will be a boy."

She frowned. "Even if it is, he shouldn't have a boy's name."

"Why not?"

"I want him, or her, to work things out for themself. Names are where the brainwashing starts."

"So what do you suggest?"

She wrinkled her beautiful nose. "Tarachand. It means 'star'. Or Ashanti."

"What does that mean?"

"'African tribe'."

The smart thing to do was run: either to his brother in Flint, or to an uncle in Lawrence. He could load his truck while she slept and then just drive for days. He'd soon find work and a new girl, but the job would be shit, and she would be poor and not so good in bed. Whenever they did it, he'd think of Skye. The way she raised her ass. How deep and tight it was. He thought about that time on the train when she was sitting on the basin and she had her legs so high and every time he pushed in her the man in the mirror did too. He thought of all the times she sucked him till his dick felt like a straw. The taste of her pussy. The clench of her ass. The idea they might never do it again made him sick and giddy. He supposed, with a losing feeling, that this was probably Love.

Skye continued building a bridge — a *golden* bridge — between the baby and her. She began keeping a birth diary addressed to the baby:

Today you gave me life. I was about to cross the street when I felt you kick. I stopped and looked and saw the mac truck and then I knew you'd saved me. Thank you, Tarachand, my love. I cannot wait to meet you.

She also wrote a series of letters to very important people:

Dear Mr. President,

I want my son/daughter to grow up in a world without hate. I want him/her to look at the sky and never feel like the clouds. Please stop the wars. Please help the whales. Please make people paint their houses orange, yellow, and pink.

Most mornings she was up early, sitting on the balcony, the new day on her belly. She looked at the ocean, its endless waves, and it did not seem vast or empty: it was one great promise.

And then there was a morning when everything seemed to stop. The sounds of dogs and lawnmowers faded. The traffic still moved, but now without noise, and everything came closer, and then it moved away. It was as if the world had taken a breath, then slowly let it out. She looked at the ocean, its waves said *Yes*, and she knew it was time.

David helped her to the truck and although it was a ten-minute drive, it felt like a Great Journey. The streets and shops seemed unfamiliar. All the signs for rooms and chicken seemed to hint at more. As if behind, inside their letters, there were other messages of truly great importance, and as the first contraction hit, the letters rippled and swam.

At the hospital they wheeled her to the room where It would happen. The walls were a beautiful green, the light was truly white. She put on a gown that copied the walls and David was there and the nurses were there and every face was kind and happy and the contractions were getting closer and closer and the doctor had a trimmed white beard and held his clipboard as if it were myrrh.

Skye refused an epidural: she would share her baby's pain. This was the right way, the natural way, the way that women since the dawn of time had bonded with their child. After Tarachand was born, she'd tell her/him about the birth, the pain of it, and he or she would laugh and say, "Mummy, I remember."

But she could feel small fingers clawing her insides. They were tearing and scraping and digging their nails in like they meant to turn her inside out and she tried to go to Teehanu where she could be with the wolves and the yaks but every time she made it there the claws just dragged her back. She looked at the doctor, then at the nurses, and she remembered their lips and eyes from when she was a child. Someone had given her a book about the lives of the martyrs. One of the saints was being tortured while the townsfolk laughed. They clustered round with mocking faces while a nurse with terrible breath was telling her to push, push harder, and when the claws pushed through her stomach she could only scream. She couldn't breathe, she was going to die. And then she felt it leave.

The doctor said, "It's a boy." The baby looked like it had been boiled. Like a doll covered in blood.

"Do you want to hold him?" the doctor said. She just shook her head.

"She's too tired," said David, and put out his hands. The baby weighed as much as a ham. It seemed inconceivable that something so weak and small would ever be able to ride a bike or throw a punch or rob a liquor store. It was like some over-sized mouse brought in by a cat and now there would be no time to drink or play pool, there would be no long afternoons with his head between her legs while she virtually spoke in tongues. No more taking from her purse. No more using her card. From now on all his time would be spent taking care of it. Stopping it from being crushed or broken, taken by mountain lions.

And this was a fucking tragedy. He'd had the perfect life. Things had been so sweet. Living by the ocean with a hot rich girl who only asked that he fuck her often and hard while keeping his big mouth shut.

As he drove home from the hospital the sun was high in the sky. The windows were open and the radio was playing this Fleetwood Mac song that he shamefully liked. The road was clear and stretched ahead and he felt pretty strange. It was like someone had opened this forgotten door in the back of his head and now all this light and air could get into these rooms that must have stank something awful because he hadn't felt like this since he saw Bambi escape from the hunters.

It wasn't till he was home and drinking that he knew what it was. Relief. It was how they felt in that Bachman story when they couldn't walk anymore. They knew they were going to be shot but, oh, how it felt to *stop*. How it felt to not have to worry whenever she got a statement or went to the bank or just put her hand in her pocket looking for the five that had been there only last night. Because from now on there'd be no need to steal. They were no longer a couple, they were a family, which meant that they'd share. He'd never need to get a job, the *baby* would be his job.

When Skye came home she saw the banner that read, "Welcome Tarachand!" She looked at the baby and felt annoyed, because it couldn't read the sign, it probably couldn't *see* the sign, but otherwise the place looked nice, the *shui* of it was right.

They sat on the couch and David held her. She had never been so tired. Her back was sore; it hurt when she pissed; her breasts were swollen, they ached. All she wanted to do was sleep. To drift slowly away.

She shut her eyes. Slowed her breath. Stepped towards another world where there was only peace. There was grass. The yak bell's *clop*. And then the baby screamed.

"Is he hungry?"

"He's *always* hungry."

She brought the baby to her breast. Its lips were like a pinch. It sucked and sucked and her milk flowed and it should have been such joy, for her to pass on Life like this, to nourish a child so it could flower and grow and learn till the blessed day when it stood on a podium and gave a speech that would move the world.

But the Life was leaving her. It was being taken.

And David had seen a lot of shit but this was freakin' awesome. He looked at the vacant nipple. He stroked the edge of her breast.

"What?"

"Huh?"

"What do you want?"

"Nothing, I was just..."

"You were just what?"

"Nothing," he said, and took back his hand. The baby continued to pinch. It sucked and drank till she was drained and then it fell asleep.

Skye, exhausted, closed her eyes. She could hear Brazilian salsa from the flat above. It swelled and laughed and shook its hips because it had no child.

When she woke it was dark. David made an alfalfa salad. They ate while the baby slept.

"I had this incredible dream," he whispered.

She swallowed some sprouts.

"I can't remember everything. But we were definitely by the sea. You and Tarachand and me. I don't know what we were doing. Maybe we were just hanging out. But there was this totally amazing feeling. There was this sort of light in us. As if we were *holy*."

Skye shrugged and continued chewing, which he guessed was fair comment. Dreams were just the TV shows your brain made while you slept. He would have forgotten it quickly — there was too much else to do — except he started getting re-runs, almost every night. Him and Skye and Tarachand. The clear and endless sea. He could look down to the Spanish galleons with their chests of gold. There were fish and octopi. A crocodile playing a harp.

He tried to talk to Skye. She was watching *Friends* while pumping milk from her breasts.

"Not now," she said, as the bottle filled. "Ross is going to ask Rachel."

She had been on the couch all week. Eating Venezuelan food while watching anything. She only held Tarachand when he cried to be fed. Then she cradled his head and whispered while he sucked at her breast. Her face was different in those moments, more like the Skye he knew.

He went into their bedroom till the show had ended.

When he came back she was feeding. The baby's hand was on her breast, her lips were by the baby's ear, and it was such a beautiful scene that he had to step closer — but quietly, so as not to disturb — and this was how he came to hear her murmur *little fuck*.

That night the dream returned with greater clarity. When he went into the lounge in the morning she was watching TV.

"Can you turn that off?"

"Why?"

"We need to talk."

"Go ahead."

David turned the TV off. Skye turned it back on. David turned it off then threw the clicker across the room.

"Listen," he said and sat down beside her. She looked at him with a bored, sulky face. He told her the dream, but she still looked bored, and then he said what he wanted to do, what they needed to do, and although she said, "That's totally dumb", he continued, because he had to, for him, for her, for Tarachand, and slowly the light in her eyes returned, that spark of *chai* or soul or whatever. He kissed her and told her he loved her, and she kissed him back and said, "OK", and that night, after she'd sucked him off, the dream did not repeat.

David took care of everything. He hired the boat and caterers. He sent out invitations. *A Celebration*, it said on the cards. *East Pier. 2p.m.*

The sun rose on a glassy sea that waited like a stage. David wore a new brown suit that made him look like Sinatra. Skye wore a series of muslin layers that spoke of her beautiful curves.

Their guests were waiting on the pier. Her friends,

their neighbours, the nurses, the doctor, everyone but her parents (dead) and his father (in jail). They climbed aboard and then set off. The sun was warm and the sea was calm and people smiled and drank champagne as the boat smoothed through the waves. They sailed till the land seemed far away, like something painted on air. The bubbles rose in the golden liquid. The baby slept in his cot.

As the boat came to a stop, David looked around. People were laughing and smiling so nicely. Skye was her beautiful self. He did not think he had ever experienced such love. It was like a warm fountain planted in his gut and this, as well as the champagne, was why he ended up making a speech. Originally he had planned to thank them for coming and then move straight to the toasts. Instead, he found himself saying that every Life was special. He said it brought new Hope. He said that young life was a beautiful question mark. He talked about the great Promise contained in every birth. He said there was nothing more exciting than watching a new Life. He thanked all the relations and friends for being in this moment with them. Then he asked them to pray, in whatever way they chose, that their beautiful son would be happy, peaceful and fulfilled throughout a long life of grace, and most of the guests lowered their heads, shut their eyes, and those who did not looked at the sea in a benevolent way.

When David said, "Thank you," they cheered. Then he tied a velvet cord around the middle of the baby. He secured it to a railing, then climbed into the small dinghy they'd towed behind. In front of everyone, beneath the kind and loving sun, the gulls who hovered like watching angels, David lowered Tarachand into the warm Pacific.

The water lapped his head. He screamed. And David, when he told the story, admitted that it sounded crazy. "You won't believe this, but it's true. That was when a shark just took him."

David watched the bubbles of blood. Someone screamed. There were shouts. This was not the dream.

He stared at the waves that were green. Curling hundred dollar bills that cusped and quickly sank. Down to the bottom. Forever.

He turned toward the screams. They were waving their arms and pointing, as if they were on some great ocean liner that was sounding its horn because, after all the farewells, all the tears, they were starting a beautiful cruise, and although David did not want to be left behind, his place was with Tarachand, or rather, where he'd been.

But the people were so good and kind that they would not give up. They called his name and stretched out their arms and he looked back one last time at the water that was only grey and thought of the shark swimming below and it did not seem evil or bad, it had only done what it must, and so great was the force of this truth that he staggered and almost fell from the dinghy. The faces cheered, or maybe screamed, and as he regained his balance he tasted salt in his mouth. Was it tears, or from the sea? Maybe both, maybe neither, and he remembered what Skye had said one day when she came back from Eco Yoga about all things being a choice and at the time he hadn't cared because he loved when her pussy was sweaty, but now, as he stepped from the dingy, climbed over the railing and onto the boat, he could hear her finish her sentence and although the people clustered round him, he didn't let them interrupt and as she spoke of *goodness* and *purpose* he pushed people out of the way more roughly than he really meant to because these were her words, they belonged to her, and, like all great treasures, they needed their rightful owner as much as she needed them and it was his duty, for her sake, for their sake, to tell her what was already swimming beneath the waves of her knowledge.

She was slumped against the mast. Her hands were over her face. When he put his arms around her, she began to sob.

"Listen to me," he said. "Remember what you used to say?"

His voice seemed high and strained and not entirely his own.

"You said that all life came from the sea."

She nodded into his chest.

"Tarachand has just gone back to where he came from. Maybe he's in the shark at the moment. But that shark will swim through the sea, and it won't stop swimming, it can't, and so he'll be all throughout the sea, and whenever we swim in the sea we'll be with him again."

She stopped crying. She raised her head. There was something in her eyes, a question that spoke of need, a voice that cried, *You're almost there*, as if he was, at long last, approaching the end of some slow race he had been competing in for months, for years, without even knowing it, a race whose prize was better than sex on trains or a fistful of green.

"If the shark hadn't eaten him — "

He did not get a chance to finish.

"Fuck the shut *up*," she said.

nature of theft:

It is, I hope, quite obvious that I did not steal this story directly from 'life'. Names and places have been altered, along with such minor details as how *the shark ate the baby: the woman who told me this story — which she claimed had happened to friends of hers — swore the shark had bitten the baby in half (toes to waist, one assumes). Although this seemed intensely dramatic, I felt it would be beyond the credence of most readers.*

stolenstories

contributor biographies

Angus Woodward

Angus Woodward, whose great-grandparents were Scottish, lives with his wife and two daughters in Baton Rouge, Louisiana. His fiction has appeared widely in US literary journals, including *Louisiana Literature*, *Xavier Review*, *Talking River Review*, *Alimentum*, and *Mochila Review*. Margaret Media published his collection of short stories, *Down at the End of the River*, in 2008.

Lindsay Bower

Lindsay Anne Bower originally hails from the armpit of the universe, otherwise known as Columbia, South Carolina. Likes: New York, thunderstorms. Dislikes: arrogance, bios. She currently lives in Edinburgh.

Ron Butlin

Ron Butlin is the Edinburgh Makar (Poet Laureate). With an international reputation as a prize-winning novelist he is one of Scotland's most acclaimed writers. His collection of short stories, *No More Angels*, was published last summer.

He lives in Edinburgh with his wife, the writer Regi Claire, and their golden retriever.

Lucille Valentine

Lucille wrote stories at school (her first published poem was in Afrikaans) and flash fiction in the back row of her engineering maths class at university. She started writing again after her first son was born. He is now seven. They moved to Newcastle upon Tyne in March 2007 from her native South Africa where her last job was with IT systems for petrol stations. Now, in addition to writing horoscopes for the bimonthly *Odyssey* magazine and as many short stories as possible, she is busy with a novel set in 1900 and writes poetry that gets published in diaries.

Rusty Harris

Rusty Harris grew up in Southern California's San Fernando Valley, the setting for her short story "One-Man Band" which was published in the 2008 edition of *Cutthroat* magazine, Volume IV. In addition to short stories, Harris has recently finished work on a middle grade novel and several picture books for children. Away from the computer, she tutors, gardens, misses hergrandchildren, and struggles with a recalcitrant tenor saxophone. Rusty Harris lives in Ventura County, California, with her husband, the musician Tony Harris.

Alison Miller

Alison Miller was born and grew up in Orkney, before leaving for university in Aberdeen. She has lived in Glasgow most of her adult life. For ten years she worked in Castlemilk for the Workers Educational Association (WEA), running writers' workshops and other classes. From there she went to the Centre for Women's Health where she set up the counselling and group work service. A graduate of the Creative Writing Course run by Strathclyde and Glasgow universities, Alison's first novel *Demo* was published by Penguin in 2006. Currently she travels between Orkney and Glasgow to work on her second novel, *Coming Back*, set in Orkney.

Sarah Salway

Sarah Salway is a short story writer, novelist, journalist and creative writing tutor based in London. Her third novel, *Getting the Picture*, will come out with Random House in Summer 2009. She spent part of her summer at the Tiny Circus arts project in Iowa, and is about to start a garden history course.

Sarah blogs at *www.sarahsalway.blogspot.com*.

Lauren Simpson

Since leaving Scotland to return to her native Birmingham, Alabama, Lauren Simpson has participated in a magazine launch, interned at *Southern Living*, taught freshman English, and appeared in an issue of *Lipstick*, a local women's monthly, with a large snake around her neck. Every so often, she also finds time to write. Her fiction has been published in *The Golden Hour Book* and *V: New International Writing from Edinburgh*.

Dinh Vong

Dinh Vong is currently a Teach for America corps member, teaching middle school ESL and Social Studies at a high-need urban school in Houston, Texas. She received her MFA in fiction at Arizona State University, where she also served as the international editor for *Hayden's Ferry Review*.

Jo Swingler

Jo Swingler was brought up in Devon and has since travelled widely in Asia, where she worked for six years as an English teacher. She spent three more years teaching in the UK before deciding to give it all up and focus completely on writing. She is now studying for the MSc in Creative Writing at Edinburgh University. Her work has been published in *Aesthetica*, *QWF* and on the *Guardian* Poetry Workshop website. She has been longlisted for the Bridport Prize and Cinnamon Press First Collection Award. One day she hopes to be shortlisted for something.

Regi Claire

Regi Claire was raised in Switzerland but currently lives in Edinburgh with her husband, the writer Ron Butlin, and their golden retriever. Regi has had two books published: *Inside~Outside* (shortlisted for the Saltire First Book Award) and The Beauty Room (longlisted for the Allen Lane/MIND Book of the Year Award) and her work has appeared in numerous literary magazines, anthologies, and on BBC Radio 4. She won the *Edinburgh Review* 10th Anniversary Short-Story Competition, was a Cadenza prize winner, and has received Bursaries from the SAC, Pro Helvetia and Thurgau Lottery Foundation, as well as a UBS Cultural Foundation Award. Regi is currently a creative writing tutor at the National Gallery of Scotland. *Fighting It*, her new collection of stories, which includes 'The Death Queue', will be published in spring 2008.

Louis E. Bourgeois

Louis E. Bourgeois teaches writing and philosophy at The University of Mississippi in Oxford. His latest collection of prose, *The Gar Diaries*, was nominated for The National Book Award in 2008. Bourgeois is also founder and editor of VOX Press.

Nicole Reid

Nicole Louise Reid is the author of the novel *In the Breeze of Passing Things* (MacAdam/Cage). Her stories have appeared in *The Southern Review*, *Quarterly West*, *Meridian*, *Black Warrior Review*, *Confrontation*, *turnrow*, *Crab Orchard*

Review, and *Grain Magazine*. She is the winner of the 2001 Willamette Award in Fiction, and has also won awards from the Pirate's Alley William Faulkner Short Story Competition and the F. Scott Fitzgerald Literary Society. She teaches creative writing at the University of Southern Indiana and is fiction editor of *Southern Indiana Review*.

Craig Bayne

Craig Bayne is a writer who lives and works in Glasgow, where he co-edits the literature and arts magazine *Are Volitional*. A graduate from Strathclyde University, he is currently working on his first novel, a parody of Dante's *Divine Comedy* set in the red light district of Amsterdam.

He can be contacted at *craig.bayne@hotmail.co.uk*.

Alison Key

Alison Key works as an editor for a national charity, but much prefers to be writing. She has been published in *Mslexia* and her story "The Ground Beneath Her Feet" won first prize in the Cinnamon Press short story award 2008. She has recently completed an MA in Creative Writing at Goldsmiths, University of London. She lives in London.

Nick Holdstock

Nick Holdstock's work has appeared in *Edinburgh Review*, *Stand* and *The Golden Hour Book*.

www.nickholdstock.com

the golden hour book

also available from forest publications

The Golden Hour is poetry and prose, it's acoustic and it's electric, it's physical and mental. The Golden Hour Book (and CD) is an effort to distil the goodness of our live performance — the words, the music, the bottles of beer and wine — into a volume of pure, unrefined Gold featuring the artists who performed over the first year of The Golden Hour. It is Golden.

The first volume of collected stories, poetry and songs from The Golden Hour captures new and fresh international voices, and the second — available in 2009 — only furthers the legacy and documents the increasing prestige of this Edinburgh institution.

Enquire for your copy at fine booksellers or order online at www.theforest.org.uk.

what is
the forest?

The Forest is a volunteer-run, collectively owned and operated arts charity based in the heart of Edinburgh. Self-funded by its vegetarian café, The Forest houses a gig space and art gallery, numerous workshops and the monthly Golden Hour reading and performance night. It provides an alternative space, free and open to all, to hold events, display art, make books and records, or just hang out, eat healthy food and meet like-minded individuals.

This book is one example of what The Forest funds. It also distributes grants to meritorious artistic and community projects. For more information, or to get involved, please visit the Forest in person or at our website: www.theforest.org.uk.